How to
DISAPPEAR

How to
DISAPPEAR

BRUNA GOMES

Encircle Publications
Farmington, Maine, U.S.A.

How to Disappear © 2021 Bruna Gomes

Paperback ISBN 13: 978-1-64599-180-9
Hardcover ISBN 13: 978-1-64599-181-6
E-book ISBN 13: 978-1-64599-182-3
Kindle ISBN 13: 978-1-64599-183-0

Editor, Encircle Publications: Michael Piekny
Book design and cover design by Deirdre Wait
Cover illustration by Bruna Gomes

Published by:

Encircle Publications
PO Box 187
Farmington, ME 04938

Visit: http://encirclepub.com
info@ encirclepub.com

Dedication

This book is dedicated to you.

Step 1

Say Nothing

YOUR MIND IS A painting, and it looks like this:
The vices and virtues of
Nihilism
(or is it boredom?)
You drop dry Cheerios into your mouth as your hips sway out of time to outdated music. The late-morning sun is streaming in through your kitchen window and it is filling the room with an overwhelmingly golden apathy. You start singing along to the lyrics, replacing the words you don't know with your own and singing loud enough so that it works. Your cheap shellac manicure clinks around your milk-less bowl of cereal and you pluck out a couple more O's, dropping them into your mouth. You turn up the music so that you can no longer hear the cars rumbling along the street below.

The sun's glow becomes even warmer. You decide today might even be a good day to wear lipstick.

You plod from the kitchen to the bathroom, the music fading behind you, and you unwrap your cotton-candy-pink hair from your bath towel. Blow dry it until it's fluffy. You line your eyes with black liquid eyeliner and dust your cheeks with blush. You rub your lips together, contemplating the righteousness of lipstick, and you decide it's as righteous as it'll ever be, and so you cover your lips with the color of rosewood. It is a rather sad attempt at fixing up your pitiful appearance. Stop trying to kid yourself. In your bedroom, you replace your sweatpants with a sundress and espadrilles. You are proud of yourself, at least, for attempting to make yourself a better person, even if it is forced and unnatural, and you are unqualified; effort is hard to come by, and it is a miracle you still retain some. You sling a tote bag onto your shoulder and leave your small apartment to bathe in the mindless sun, locking the door behind you.

❧   ❧   ❧

While you are searching for your reading glasses, the home phone's ringtone shrills throughout the apartment. Cravat is the only one that ever calls you on your home phone and this time you know better than to ignore it. You put your search on hold and pick it up.

"Hello?"

"If you don't get yourself down here in ten minutes, I'm firing you."

"Okay."

"And don't even think about coming up with an excuse."

"Okay."

You put the phone back down in the handset. You are not in the mood for wearing an apron and waiting on obnoxious, perfumed people, and you're certainly not in the mood for satisfying Cravat's orders, no siree Bob, not today. You'd much prefer to find your reading glasses and sit down with a cup of lime and ginger tea and one of the second-hand books you bought last Thursday that are piled in a stack in the corner of your bedroom. It is easier to give into your worthlessness than to pretend it doesn't exist.

Ten minutes later, and still no sign of your glasses, the home phone rings again. You pick it up and bring it to your ear. "You're fired," spits Cravat. You can almost feel his saliva spray through the receiver.

"Cool beans."

"Don't bother coming back, you hear me?"

"Loud and clear, boss."

"Go and waste someone else's time."

"Will do."

Cravat manages to hang up before you do.

You have enough savings to keep you afloat for a couple months, so keep your damn chin up. Everything is fine. Don't you dare start acting like it isn't.

Please, do not fall apart.

Not again.

You finally find your glasses in your undies draw. You pick up the oversized round frames and push them up the bridge of your nose. Much better. While you read your battered copy of *The Great Gatsby*, your phone vibrates with a text from Winnie. It almost made you spill your tea.

The Shack at 8?

You don't see why not.

See you there x

You look up at the clock; it is three in the afternoon. You contemplate doing some exercise, possibly bring out the yoga mat. Exercise, though, requires the intention of gaining self-improvement—you left those intentions behind long ago. Now your body is vacant. You know that there are seventeen unread e-mails sitting in your inbox and you know that you should really use the time to reply to them. Your laptop is sitting on your unmade bed, waiting for you. The people who sent the e-mails are waiting for you. On the other hand, though, you would quite like to sit by the kitchen window and see if the tabby cat stalks by. You could even drop some food down for it. But you can't help but admit that seventeen people do outweigh one cat, and therefore it is a much more sensible decision to answer those e-mails. You retrieve your laptop from your bed and return to your position on the couch. Look at you, making smart executive decisions that you know are properly beneficial and not a waste of time. Good job. You open your mail. Three of them are subscription newsletters. At least you don't have to reply to them. Eight are from Cravat. You're not even sure he'd want you to answer them, to be completely honest. You should probably answer one, though, even if it's just for fun. There's one from Cille with a collection of files attached, and a couple of notices from your landlord. The rest are from your aunt, each of them detailing different job opportunities. You leave them, unopened. You are good at leaving things, just like things are good at leaving you.

Your best friend, it seems, is evasion.

❧ ❦ ❧

It is 7:45 and the sun has well and truly gone to sleep, but the night's air is still warm and sweet. You throw a light knitted cardigan over your dress and after redundantly reapplying your lipstick, you make your way down the apartment block and onto the street. It takes you nine minutes to walk to The Shack, a small, greasy fish and chip shop filled with tourists and bored teens, and when you arrive, you take the liberty of ordering for both yourself and Winnie. You take a seat outside while you wait for Winnie and the food, the ocean breeze gently gliding over your bare legs. Winnie arrives at

8:06, sporting her apron from the restaurant and dark circles under her eyes. She has tried to compensate by smothering her lips with lip gloss, you can tell. She eats a chip before she even greets you.

"You're toast, you know?" she finally blurts.

"Well, yeah, people who get fired aren't bread."

"Wait, he fired you?"

"Mm-hmm."

"Sheesh."

"What happened at the restaurant?"

"Oh, you should've seen it," she exclaims, clutching a chip like a cigarette, "he went completely off his head. I mean, like, totally off the rails. I'm pretty sure his mouth was even foaming. And you wanna know the worst part?"

"What's the worst part?"

"He was wearing the cravat with the tiny pink socks on it."

You nod.

"Yep. It was the ghastliest thing." She sits back in her chair and stabs her fork into a shriveled fillet of battered fish.

Winnie is a spontaneous Casanova with an eye for bargains and a smile full of whiskey. She always wears Delta Goodrem's perfume but never listens to Delta Goodrem's songs. You've been her friend since tenth grade in high school. When you got a job as a waitress at The Orchard six months ago, she decided she would do the same thing. You didn't think she'd get the job, but here she is, still employed and earning an income. Whether she is financially stable is an entirely different question altogether. You usually pay for her meals, and she usually points you to warehouse sales. Your friendship is a win-win situation. This is the first time you've ever been in a win-win situation. It is more mundane than it sounds.

"So, whatcha gonna do now?" she asks as she licks oil and salt off her fingers.

"I haven't really put much thought to it, to be honest."

"You could always go back to uni, you know, if you're desperate. You still got that student loan, right?"

"Meh."

"You didn't!"

"If it makes you feel any better, Cille keeps sending me crap to convince me to go back."

"Wait, who's Cille again?" She wrinkles her eyebrows as she tries to remember. You roll your eyes. You're pretty sure you've told her who Cille is fourteen times, give or take.

"Cille was my roommate at uni. I'm not going to bother telling you these things if you're not even going to remember."

"Oh, boo hoo. Well you gotta do something. You can't sit in that minuscule apartment of yours for the rest of your precious youth."

But you think this sounds like a great idea. You tell Winnie she should get fired too so you can both spend more time at each other's apartments.

There's a short silence while Winnie sucks on the leftover slice of lemon and thinks of the possibilities.

"Try it," you say.

She notices your lipstick is from Sephora and says, "Sephora never has sales."

❦   ❦   ❦

The next morning you wake up and it is hot, sticky, like the bowels of a rainforest. The heat drains out any energy that your sleep might have given you. You pad to the kitchen, stick your hand into the open bag of cereal, pull out a fistful and stuff them into your mouth. The sun is streaming through the window and turning the kitchen into an oven. If you wanted, you could sit very still and you would roast alive.

You go back into your bedroom and change into a white bikini and you pile your pink hair into a topknot. You grab a second-hand book from the skewed pile next to your bed and your specs and you bring it with you to the bathroom. You bend down and sprawl your limbs across the chipped green tiles, pressing your bare skin against their cool surfaces. This is a good spot to contemplate the contents of your aunt's e-mails, and whether the jobs might accept such a pathetically incompetent girl like yourself.

There isn't enough room to stretch out your legs completely, and your scapulae have become uncomfortably present. Nevertheless, it is blissful. You can feel the beads of sweat that were clinging onto your skin retreat into your pores, and the green tiles beneath you become your best friend. They are soothing, they are relieving, just as any best friend should be. More than anything, you want to be the type of girl who replies to her e-mails punctually and wakes up every morning with purpose, a girl who doesn't mind her reflection in the mirror. It is the ultimate itch that you cannot scratch; it is the scarab beetle that resides within the nape of your neck that gnaws at the edge of your brain—self-love. You understand it to be an ancient myth that you have no evidence of being real. All you have is a sweaty corpse with an insect infestation, mummified in a bikini, waiting to be resurrected by the gods. While you wait for this, you open your book above your face and begin to read.

⚜ ⚜ ⚜

It is two in the afternoon and your back has cramped up. You sit up and listen to it crack as you bend it back and forth. Your bottom is so numb that you're not even sure you can get up. You do, though, and sweat is already re-emerging out of your pores and settling on your skin in a salty slime. You long to press your cheek against the tiles again, just once more, but they've all warmed under your skin. Such oppressive heat is truly unnecessary, you decide, especially in this day and age. You don't have air-con, but the library has air-con, though. Maybe you should go there.

You pull on your sundress over your bikini, shove your feet into flip-flops and pull your hair out of its bun so that it falls just short of your shoulders. You grab your bag and head down to the street, where you walk to the closest bus stop.

The bus is empty except for an old lady that smells of kitty-pee, and a little boy with a scooter and a runny nose. You reach into your bag and offer the boy a tissue. He tugs it out of your hand and pokes out his tongue, his face scrunching up into a cute, angry ball. He blows his nose, tucks the tissue into his pocket, and then digs his index finger up his nostril and wriggles it around until he manages to pull out a funky yellow blob. The boy smiles and pops it in his mouth. You wonder what kind of mother raises such an ape.

Shut up.

How dare you mention the word *mother*.

Shut up and move on.

The bus stops a block away from the library and you hop off onto the sidewalk. As you walk to the library, you make sure to avoid stepping on the cracks.

"Hi, darl," greets the librarian as you push open the heavy glass door. Her eyes are magnified behind thick spectacles, the pearl chain caught between folds of skin along her neck. She's very short, very sweet, and very well-read.

"Hey, Mrs June. It's a hell-scape today, huh?"

"Oh, it's dreadful! Bill and Paul came in after their swim and tracked water all over the darn place! You'd think they'd have more common sense than that at their ripe age."

"You know, Mrs June, if I didn't know any better, I'd say they were probably just trying to get your attention." You stand by the counter as you wait for her reply. Her little mouth drops open and her glasses slide ever so slightly down the bridge of her nose.

"Oh, heavens! Where do you youngsters get such absurd ideas!"

You slink off into the aisles of books before she can tut at you any longer.

You like libraries, you really do, especially this one, but you wish they smelled the same as second-hand bookshops. That melancholic, dusty smell is among one of your favorites, along with lavender, and lemon verbena. That smell has a power of its own that transports you to a far-away moment and enhances the present moment at the exact same time. It's almost like magic. But you will have to make do without it for the time being. You pick a Jane Austen classic off the shelf—*Persuasion*—and you take it with you to an arm chair that is made of the type of fabric that makes your skin itch. You'll have to make do with that, too. People make do with a lot of things. You admire them. The sun is fully in the library as well and has become the day's antagonist. Sometimes you wish you had the sun's audacity, you know, to be the protagonist one day and the antagonist the next. The coolest bit is that the people don't even notice—to them the sun is still the sun, the only difference is the number on the weather report. It would be nice to be like the sun, you decide, it really would.

Your mother was like the sun.

I SAID SHUT UP.

❧　❧　❧

Someone taps you on the shoulder and you jump. Mrs June is in front of you with her glasses hanging around her neck on a pearl chain and her handbag propped on her shoulder. "We're closing now, darl," she croons.

"Already?"

"It's six o'clock. We always close at six, you of all people know that." Woah. You completely lost track of time. "I can give you a lift if you want. I know how busy the buses are now with all those youngsters getting home from work."

Mrs. June is a sweetie.

Mrs. June owns an old silver Subaru that you have been in six times before. It is exactly what one would expect of an old lady, but that is why you like it so much. "You have plans for dinner, darl?" she asks as you sit in the rumbling traffic. The mention of food reminds you that you haven't eaten all day. In fact, it has only occurred to you now that you're starving. But you know that if you tell Mrs. June of your plan-less evening, she'll insist on you joining her, and you know all too well that her insistence is the stubborn kind.

"I'm actually having dinner with an old friend, Cille."

"That's lovely, darl. Where do you youngsters eat these days?"

"Oh, you know, wherever the food is good and the drinks are cheap."

"I see."

Once you thank Mrs. June profusely for the ride home and hop out of her Subaru, you get out your phone and call Cille. You must go through with your plan so you can tell Mrs. June how the dinner was the next time you see her, because you are certain she'll ask. Cille picks up on the third ring. "Cille?"

"Yeah, hey, what's up?"

"I was thinking we could have dinner tonight. We haven't seen each other in ages."

"But it's Wednesday."

"So?"

Cille hesitates within the silence that follows.

"Fine. Where at?"

"You can choose."

More silence.

"I'll just meet you below your apartment in, like, half an hour, okay?"

You tell Cille she is a princess.

"I know."

❧   ❧   ❧

In your apartment, you quickly change out of your bikini

and dress and you throw on a white linen button-up and a brown corduroy skirt. You shove your feet into your espadrilles by the door, quickly brush your hair, and fill in your eyebrows. And then you're back down on the footpath, waiting.

Cille is the type of person who knows the difference between parsley and coriander, even though she never cooks. She likes to curse in French and reads *The Morning Herald*, and you're pretty sure her parents pay everything for her, but she's never admitted it.

When Cille arrives, you quickly peck each other on both cheeks and complain about the hot weather. She tells you to keep up as she walks quickly through Bondi. She stops at an ATM, and you're both in such a rush that you seem to forget what common decency is and you find yourself right there standing next to her as she punches her Pin number into the keypad.

Three, seven, two, six.

You both continue walking until you reach a little Italian restaurant with red-and-white checked tablecloths. Once you've both ordered, Cille finally relaxes.

"So, how's life going?"

"Pretty much same old me."

"Did you get those e-mails I sent you?"

"I did, thanks."

"Your roots are growing back. You should just go back to your natural color, you were so pretty when your hair was brown."

"I don't have the sort of time to be spending hours in salons, you know."

"*Ta gueule*, you don't do a thing."

You gather she has a point.

"I'll only believe you when you come back to uni."

"Well then I guess you'll never believe me."

The waiter comes with your food and you both eat silently, relieved for a reason to shut up. When Cille finishes her pasta, she gets up to go to the restroom. Her wallet, you seem to notice, is right there across from you on the table. You could touch it if you reached out. So, you do reach out. And you touch it. You've come this far, so you may as well pick it up. You undo the chic zipper. A thick wad of cash fills one of the pockets, the notes pristine and powerful. Surely if you examined one, Cille wouldn't mind. Don't look around the restaurant for onlookers or you'll make it more obvious.

Ok, maybe just a small glance.

But make it quick.

Is that a security camera? No, just a speaker. The music is quite nice.

The coast is clear. You let your fingers walk along the tops of the notes. They're crisp, straight from the bank, as if Cille brought them just for you. You hold onto a twenty. Wait, no, go for the fifty. You pluck it out and stuff it into your bra. You're about to zip the wallet back up, but convince yourself you need her credit card.

Three, seven, two, six.

Three, seven, two, six could get you some more cash.

You add the credit card to your bra and put everything back the way it was. When Cille gets back from the restroom, she complains about the poor sanitation of public toilets.

Once Cille decides she needs to go to bed quick-smart, she calls the waiter for the bill.

"I'll pay," you tell her, "I'm the one that dragged you out here anyway."

"*Merde*, I don't think I've ever seen you pay for anything."

"Yeah, of course." The waiter brings over the card machine and you pull out your card from your own wallet. You pray it won't get declined. When the payment goes through, Cille thanks you for a lovely night and you both depart on your merry ways.

On your way back to your apartment, you stop at an ATM. You stick Cille's card into the slot and press three, seven, two, six. You withdraw two thousand dollars. You walk around the block, keeping your stride calm and classy, find another ATM, and withdraw another two thousand. As you keep going on your way back home, you hurriedly drop the card into a bin on the footpath. In your apartment, you stuff the notes into your pillow case, put on your pajamas, and brush your teeth. As you stare at your reflection in the dirty mirror above the small vanity, you can't stop thinking about how much you hate what you see. Obnoxious pink hair falling limp around your shoulders, a caramel complexion that you're too scared to be proud of. Wide eyes and chapped lips.

You hate it, you hate her, you spit at your reflection.

You've drowned yourself in your own saliva.

❦   ❦   ❦

The next morning you are woken up by your phone's ringtone, and it lights up with Cille's name. You brace yourself before answering.

"Have you seen my credit card?"

You sit up and contemplate your answer. "No. Why?"

"I can't find it."

"I can look through my things if you want."

"Thank you!"

"Hold up. Let me get out of bed. Okay, I'm up." You get up and walk over to the kitchen, where you pour yourself a glass of water and lean on the part of the bench that is drenched in sunlight. You are once again aglow with the potential for heroism. You come up with something exquisite: "Did you leave it in the ATM?"

"*Merde.*"

"Go ahead and cancel it."

Cille hangs up at that remark.

You are about to go back to bed to continue sleeping, repulsed by the thought of having to present yourself to anyone, but a sudden knock at the door stops you. You weren't expecting anyone, were you? Maybe Cille called the police, maybe the phone call didn't quite put her suspicions to rest. You open the door to find Alejandro standing on your doorstep.

His curls of beautiful brown hair twist in every direction, and his T-shirt is sporting a tiny hole just below the neckline, mocking his own filthy wealth. He looks beautiful, but you wouldn't dare admit it. In fact, his undeniable beauty has officially ruined your morning. He is not beautiful. He is dangerous. It is an undeniable danger.

You had done so well at pretending you had forgotten about him. You pretended that his unexplained absences and stashed sealed packages were a fever dream, pretended that you were never faced by his boss banging on the door, pistol loaded. You had even tried to convince yourself that you'd forgotten his name. But there he is, in the most tangible and unavoidable way possible, smelling of the fabric-softener you could only describe as Alejandro's Scent. "How was your field trip with your boss?" you bite. You can tell that the bite went through his skin, and it bugs you that he doesn't bite back. Your morning has already been ruined, so you really wouldn't mind a battle of wits. Instead of accepting your challenge, he says,

"How do you always manage to look so pretty? Even this early in the morning?" His accented voice is quiet. Maybe he isn't sure if his words will be accepted by you.

"What are you doing here, Alejandro." You cross your arms to cover your pajama top.

He says he misses you, misses you quite a lot, and swoons over your pink hair like a boy at a lolly store, eyeing out the cotton candy. The way he looks at you is almost as if he's asking for your permission. When you don't say anything, he leans forward and begins to enfold you in one of his heavenly hugs, a hug that you have been deprived of for six whole months. He nestles his nose into your hair and you can feel him take in the smell of your conditioner. And then, almost without realizing, you slide your hand up his threadbare T-shirt and you rest it on the small of his back, where his smooth skin dips at the spine. It makes your heart beat all silly. Or maybe your heart is caving and needs you to know this.

What kind of a girl are you to let a boy make your heart feel embarrassed? A weak one, it appears.

In return, Alejandro sprinkles delicate little kisses atop your head, then down onto your forehead, and onto your cheek. You slide your other hand up the front of his shirt, and you let your hand glide over the planes of his chest. Or rather, he lets you. And somehow, his kisses end up on your lips. How did you come to kissing Alejandro in your doorframe?

You are weak, but you are also wanted.

You have traded your strength for attention. Again. That is the last thing you expected to happen on this Thursday morning. Why haven't you learned your lesson?

You grab him by the hand and lead him to your kitchen, and you both lean into the narrow stream of sunlight, giving in to your invincible hunger for each other as if disaster was something to be hungry for. You guess you are both making the most of this unscheduled occurrence, like when you come across a good song you haven't heard in a while. You want to listen to it until you get sick of it all over again.

And then a cloud floats over the sun and the spot you were tangled together in is no longer warm, so you let go of him.

How dare he treat you like he does, you tell him, your voice wavering for control.

He promises that you'll talk about it later. You don't want a 'later' with him. He smooths your hair out of your face and pecks your nose lightly. You shake him off.

"That's unfair." You cross your arms, conscious of your braless chest under your thin pajamas.

"Then you want me to leave?" He smiles as if your ruined morning is somehow his amusement. Another one of his games.

If only you had read about someone making out in the kitchen in one of your books, then this would be familiar territory. His lips perfectly hold cupid's arrow. You reply by wrapping your hand around the back of his neck and pulling his lips to yours.

His kisses make you want to cry.

❧   ❧   ❧

Later that day you go out to the supermarket for your monthly shop. You leave Alejandro sprawled across your couch, asleep, a little boy enjoying his nap hour. Before leaving you nicked a fresh twenty-dollar note from his wallet; something for the numerous hours you had spent crying over him.

When you have all your groceries, you are about to walk back to your apartment, but you stop. Something is not right. Alejandro is waiting for you. You can picture him sleeping, his sculpted body taking up most of the living room like decor. But the idea of going back there suddenly feels stifling, and not just because of him. You step to one side of the footpath, lean against a lamppost. You cannot go back, not now, not ever. Why keep a flower in the same soil that lets it die over and over again? So what if you just walk away? Sure, there are a couple of unread books and some nice clothes, but you can find the exact same books elsewhere, buy new clothes from knock-over boutiques. The four thousand dollars from last night are in your wallet; you basically have everything you need. To hell with it. You need new soil to plant your problems into. You want a new sarcophagus, one that is elaborately decorated with symbols that are designed to rejuvenate you into a girl worthy of defining herself as a deity, painted in gold and royal blue. You do not want to go back to your crumby apartment. Your apartment is where girls go to lose their self-esteem and forget to water their flowerpots. The corners of every room reek of disappointment and you are so tired of holding your nose.

Instead of going back to yours, you go to Winnie's place.

You're probably doing your landlord a favor, anyway.

When you get to Winnie's townhouse, you knock on the door and wait for a reply, which doesn't come. There are three parched pot plants on the porch, and you figure that one of them must have a spare key underneath it, because Winnie isn't creative enough to think of a better system. Sure enough, you check under the second pot and there is the key. You use it to let yourself in. You've never actually been inside her house before, and you're surprised by how pretty and elegant it is. You were expecting collections of dirty mugs and bare, chipped walls, but no, what you are greeted by is marble bench tops and framed abstract art. It was a house that you'd expect someone like Cille to live in, not Winnie. You put your groceries away in her pantry and water the plants outside.

A couple of hours later Winnie arrives in her waitress attire, her hair limp and her mascara smudged. When she sees you in the living room popping grapes into your mouth and flicking through the magazine you found lying on the coffee table, she screams.

"I got bored of my place so I came to join you," you explain.

"You could've at least called. Wait. How did you get in? If you broke the lock, then you'll be paying for repairs. I'm not dishing out a single cent."

"I found your spare key."

Winnie looks at you, confused.

"It's okay if I stay, right? Why didn't you ever tell me how lovely your house is?" Winnie shrugs, looking around.

"I guess it never really came up. It's not much, anyway."

You wish she would stop being humble, it is annoying you because of how false it is.

"Just chuck some pillows and a blanket on the couch. I'm going to take a shower. There are pajamas in my wardrobe and frozen lasagna from The Orchard in the freezer that you can put in the microwave. You can have a shower after me but you can't use my L'occitane lemon verbena body wash."

When you look at the soggy square of lasagna that was clearly only meant to be enjoyed by one person, you feel bad. You are a burden, a heavy sack that you have heaved into Winnie's home, filled with lumps of rock and unfulfilled expectations. Your phone keeps ringing, Alejandro's name lighting up your screen, and you stare at it until the noise stops. Once Winnie is out of the shower, you hop in, and you lather the lemon verbena body wash all over you until you could be mistaken for the plant itself. Your phone continues to light up with texts from Alejandro.

> If you're not here in the next 10 mins I'm leaving
>
> Come back
>
> Where are you

I'm warning you, I'll go

I'm gone. Don't try to find me at your
apartment.

Text me

Please

While sharing the lasagna on Winnie's cream leather
couch, she tells you of Cravat's incompetence in being a
member of the human race, and how he would be much
better off if he befriended skunks, or even puffer fish.
She tells you of the immensity of her savings as a result
of shopping at Vinnies, and how she started wearing
Rihanna's scent instead of Delta Goodrem's, because it
makes her feel more cultured. When she finally takes a
breath to wipe the tomato sauce off her plate with her
index finger, you decide that you are jealous of her. At
least, you think that that's the way to describe it. You
envy her Persian rug and her bamboo aroma diffuser;
you convince yourself the rug must be imitation-Persian.
Maybe if you'd known she had all this, you wouldn't have
been compelled to be so surprised.

❧   ❧   ❧

The next morning you leave the house while Winnie is
still asleep. The first stop you make is the bank, where
you put the four thousand dollars into your account. You
then quickly stop by your apartment and pick up your
passport. Next, you go to the travel agency. You ponder

over the list of specials, deciding which place would contain the fewest people that know your name. You finally settle on New York. The travel agent helps you book a ticket for tonight, which she questions multiple times and every time you assure her, yes, you would like to fly tonight. Maybe she doesn't take your pink hair seriously.

By five p.m. you're at the airport, stuffing a mustard-clad hot dog into your lipstick-deprived mouth, waiting for the loudspeaker to call your flight. When your phone buzzes with texts and missed calls from both Alejandro and Winnie, you turn the damn thing completely off.

Step 2

Become a Stranger

THE AIR IN NEW York is decisively different to that of Bondi, and you breathe in as much of it as possible in an attempt to acquaint yourself with the area. When leaving the airport, you asked the taxi driver to take you to the cheapest part of Manhattan to look for hotels, and as you slowly trundle along in the choked traffic, you peer at all the streets with unfamiliar names, which is utterly satisfying. In fact, you almost feel lost, and you wish that the streets didn't have signs so that you could never be found, like a misplaced earring. The buildings are tall and brave and angular, nothing like the stout, amiable ones in Bondi, and they loom above you watching in curiosity.

The sidewalks are bustling with fleets of men wearing trench coats and women with thin eyebrows, all of them walking in urban symmetry. It is very soothing to watch. Soon enough a shard of green in the corner of your peripheral vision slices through the grey landscape, and you squeal in delight.

"Central Park!" you shrill, pressing your oily nose against the taxi's window.

"Indeed, it is, ma'am," replies the driver, his accent thick and luxurious.

"Would you like me to stop?" He pronounces 'stop' as 'stawp', and it makes your heart skip a beat.

"Oh, if you don't mind."

The driver pulls over and you leap out of the cab and onto the grass. The grass is different here, too, just like the air. The trees are friendly and welcoming. You cannot help but smile. When you hop back into the cab, you say,

"It's all quite magical."

"Maybe if you're not from here."

But while you observe the way a man unwraps his oversized sandwich on a park bench, a pickle falling onto his lap, and his handheld radio at full volume, disrupting everyone around him, you disagree with the driver. It is incredibly magical.

The cabbie drops you off at a rundown building, its walls crumbling onto the footpath. You walk in, the only luggage with you being your tote bag, and ask for a room. "Preferably with a view," you add.

The man behind the desk tells you there are no rooms with views.

When you pay, you are reminded of the sparse amount of money that is populating your bank account. You climb the steep, narrow staircase to the top floor, the paint rubbing onto the soles of your shoes. Your room, which does not actually lock properly, consists of a plastic chair, a rusty cot, and a window that looks as if it has been repeatedly broken. Looking out of it you can see into someone's bathroom in the next building—not what you were hoping for. When you sit in the chair, one of the legs buckles under your weight, and so you relocate to the bed; the springs in the mattress screech under the pressure, accusing you of being heavy. This just won't do. Not in New York. You should be somewhere high up, so high that it requires an accomplished lift operator and a decent security system. For that to come true you know you will need more money, soon.

You turn your phone back on and it attacks you with missed phone calls and texts from Winnie and Alejandro, and even Cille, still complaining about her credit card. You decide to call Alejandro. If you're going to be honest with yourself, you don't actually know that much about him, just that he has a Spanish accent that makes you swoon helplessly and a loaded bank account that leaves you with an abundance of questions, but that just adds to his mystique, so you don't mind that the questions are unanswered. After you dial his number, he picks up on the second ring.

"Where are you?" he hisses through the speaker.

"Relax, Alejo, baby, don't worry about me, ok? I just need your help."

"How am I supposed to relax if I don't know where you are?"

What a funny thing to be said by a man that did the exact same thing to you six months ago.

"Well that's just the problem, you see. I'm a bit far from Bondi right now and I need money to get back. I'm just in a bit of a pickle, is all. All you need to do is transfer a bit into my bank account and I'll be there with you in no time."

"How much money?" You think for a second before answering. How much really is an apartment in New York City? It must be furnished, too, of course. "I'd say about seven million."

"Be serious for once. How much money do you need?" the way his accent stresses the syllables is delightful, making you sigh ever so softly.

"Maybe seventy-five thousand. Look, just slide that money into my account, make yourself comfortable in my apartment, and I'll be there before you know it. You can even buy silk sheets for the bed, if you want. And change the light switch in the bedroom so it does that dimming thing, you know?"

"Champagne, too?"

"Fill the entire fridge with it."

"And you promise you'll be back?" *Prrromeese*.

"Sure!" You hang up and sit on the horrible bed as you wait for the notification signifying the transfer.

Finally, *ping, you have just been transferred $75,000 from Alejandro Escamilla,* and you let yourself sleep, making sure the grubby sheets avoid your even grubbier face.

❧   ❀   ❧

The following morning, Friday, no wait, Saturday—really, you're not sure which one—you wake up to the song of a construction site. How charming. When you hop out of bed your stomach caves in, demanding food. You swat it and tell it to toughen up. Suddenly, the northern hemisphere's temperature slaps you in the face, cold and sharp, and you foolishly regret not bringing a coat with you.

You head down to reception, such as it is, tote in tow, and you ask the receptionist in a smooth, sweet voice that you only ever save for men with accents if you could pretty-please borrow his coat, just for the morning. When you make a show of rubbing your bare arms and scrunching your eyebrows into a knot of self-pity he gives in and hands it over. You thank him and slide it on. It smells of dusty linen and sad stories.

As you walk along the bustling city streets, you decide that whatever apartment you choose must be better than Winnie's house. You need to do better than Winnie. And Cille. And if that entails eating foods that you do not know how to pronounce, then so be it. The sun is smiling down on you, and because you forgot to bring your headphones, you hum a song to yourself, the melody softens everything about you and you smile. Oh, how spontaneous you feel in this very moment. The sensation is so lovely that you begin to fear how it could vanish.

Just like love.

Just like Alejandro.

Just like money.

Every now and again you receive a judgmental glare that's lathered in mascara and paired with a raised, plucked eyebrow. The glances are swiftly carried away by lean, legging-clad legs. It doesn't bother you; you know all too well that your pink hair does a good job at repelling serious people. You do wish you had a lipstick, though, to make your lips look more kissable. Your lips will just have to make do with a smile for now.

Eventually, you come across a tall building with sparkling windows and the stature of a flight attendant. By the front door is a sign emblazoned with 'Now Leasing,' so you make your way into the lobby. A chandelier immediately grabs your attention. The light refracting off the delicate crystals is winking at you flirtatiously. Absolutely grand, the chandelier. Grander than anything Cille could ever own. The upholstery is plush and alluring. In fact, you never knew until now just how alluring a couch could be. At the far end of the lobby, the desk stands proudly, the receptionist standing even prouder in his pressed suit, a well-practiced smirk settled firmly on his face.

"What can I help you with, ma'am?" he asks as you

approach him, looking you up and down, deciphering whether you are worthy of this impeccable place.

"I'm interested in the apartment for rent."

"You'll have to make further inquiries within the real estate agency, I'm afraid."

His general American accent bores you, and you consider giving up on the apartment then and there. You push on.

"And what's the best way I should do that, sir?" The receptionist flicks his wrist out from his sleeve and peers at his watch. His hand, you notice, is beautifully carved of smooth skin and delicate veins, a hand that you wouldn't mind holding. In fact, now that you're paying attention to him, he's visually quite enjoyable. You like the scruffy stubble on his face against his neat suit.

"The real estate agent will be here in two hours. You can wait for her if you're not short on time."

"Oh, no, I have all day."

"Very well then. Please make yourself comfortable on a seat and I'll bring you a coffee in just a moment."

Your stomach claps with relief at the mention of coffee.

Exactly two hours later, a lady with shiny, sleek, and awfully robust hair, and a narcissistic stride, struts into the lobby, bearing a stack of paperwork and an expensive coffee.

"The keys, Richmond," she orders the receptionist as she approaches the desk.

"Ah, hello, Sharon. There's a woman already here who

would like to view the apartment," he nods over to your direction. Sharon looks over, frowns in stern disapproval (you are a letdown to her), then takes the keys from Richmond's hand. She marches right toward you.

"Did you make an appointment?" she states. She smells like Chinese take-out actually. You shake your head, your oily pink hair swishing with it. You feel Sharon's gaze sweep across your locks, assessing them. You can tell she is skeptical of your disposable income. But you know that if you were her, you'd be thinking the exact same thing, even though your pink hair is only a reflection of your personality and not your credit card. If you had chosen to do your hair according to your ability to buy this apartment, you would dye it black, like the fur of a witch's cat, and it would be straight and only inflict logical thoughts. You stare at her, waiting, not bothering to think up an excuse. "Very well," she finally sighs, "we will have to make it snappy, though, because I have clients coming in fifteen minutes, clients whose lingerie cost more than your whole outfit."

And with that, you follow her into a lift that is accessorized with a lift-operator, and you all venture up to the fortieth floor. The corridor is to die for, you decide. The carpets are plush and the side-boards hold vases with real flowers. You've never been able to keep real flowers alive in vases. It takes too much love and attention. One time you got bored of the pattern on the vase so you threw the whole thing into the garbage. It was just after the garbage man had come so you could hear the vase cry when it hit the bottom of the bin. When you peered into the bin you thought you saw yourself in there, but after your gaze adjusted you just saw the crying vase and scattered petals. You assume the building's janitors will look after these flowers, and all you need to do is walk past them and think about how pretty they are.

When Sharon unlocks the front door of the apartment and you walk into the living room, it is love at first sight. The floorboards are polished to the point that you can see your own unfortunate reflection when you look down. Center stage is a luxurious Persian rug, and you can immediately tell it's authentic—you just know it. Surrounding it are two leather couches, the leather softer than any baby's bum, more wrinkled that any sun-drenched retiree. When you run your fingers along the edge of the armrest, you sigh in disbelief. The back wall of the living room is one big bookshelf, filled with the glorious spines of novel after novel, filling the room with stories waiting to be marveled at and scrutinized. And the wall opposing it isn't a wall at all. It is floor-to-ceiling glass that gives way to the most spectacular view you have ever seen. New York City's skyline stands tall and proud in front of you, its chest puffed and shoulders pushed back. You can't help but feel proud of yourself.

Look at what you have achieved. Look at how far you've come. With stolen money, but that's not the point. Just enjoy the view. You slowly continue to turn, gasp in delight when you see the grand piano in the corner of the room, sitting royally like Mozart's piano. You try to remember if they were called pianos back then. It doesn't matter that you don't actually know how to play piano; it's presence is enough to make you feel sensational. You can just pretend someone is playing it. Like Richmond, the receptionist, with his big, safe hands. Ah, yes, you can hear the soft notes already, caressing your ears. It is bliss.

It suddenly becomes apparent to you that Sharon is tap-tapping the toe of her high-heels on the floorboards impatiently, and after you mutter a small and unfelt apology, she suggests that you wrap it up. But that's fine by you—you don't need to go to the bedroom or the bathroom, or even the kitchen to know that you want this apartment, you really want it. Just as Sharon is placing her perfectly manicured hand on the front door knob, you splutter,

"I'll rent it."

"I'm sorry?"

She looks back at you, undeniably irritated. And then she throws her shiny head back and laughs, her hair making patronizing swishes.

"I'm taking the apartment," you try again, this time crossing your arms lamely.

"This unit is being leased at $68,000 per month." She removes her hand from the door knob and eyes you with profound curiosity, as if you just burped.

"Cheaper than I was expecting. Wonderful."

After a few more seconds of her elegant silence, Sharon straightens her blazer and flicks hair behind her shoulders.

"Well then," she says, not quite making eye contact, "let's go down to the office, I suppose."

❦ ❦ ❦

Half an hour later you are in Sharon's office in the real estate agency, watching her squirt hand sanitizer into her palm. Once she's finished, she displays a binder of paperwork in front of you and points to a ballpoint pen on her desk. "Fill everything in," she orders. "Don't leave anything out and don't obscure details." You nod, pick up the pen, put on your specs, and read. You are already stumped by the first section.

You need to write your name. Your full name. You weren't planning on giving your name to anyone. You thought you could rent an apartment without a name. You must've seen it in a movie before, or read it in a book. You look up at Sharon, who is eyeballing you with pungent distrust. No, you definitely need to write your name.

Good lord.

Slowly, you write out your details, something you haven't done in a very long time; when you booked your plane ticket you just got the travel agent to do it all for you. Now the pen is in your own hands. By the time all the pages have been read through by Sharon, twice, her fingers itching to point out a flaw, you are exhausted. Writing about yourself is a draining task, and you make a mental note to never do it again, unless it's vital to your ability to stay alive. You need not even perform any heavy financial lifting; you've given them your "banking information" and rent will simply be debited from your account. It sounded so elegant. *Oh, why, yes please. Just debit it from the account.*

Sharon leaves you sitting by yourself in her office for what feels like hours, giving you an abundance of unnecessary time to daydream about that grand piano in the apartment accompanied by Richmond's lovely hands. Finally, she comes back, her glossy lips pursed with disgust, and a key held between her polished fingertips.

"It's all yours."

"Woo!" you spew out, your voice wobbly. Idiot, this is why you should avoid talking to people as much as possible, to avoid uncomfortable word vomit such as this.

"Also," Sharon declares, "you should drink coffee from a straw so that it doesn't stain your teeth." Ah, now *this* is why you should avoid talking to people.

❦ ❦ ❦

You are sitting cross-legged on your divine leather couch, book in hand, the city lights sparkling in the reflection of your glasses. It is so perfect that you are almost scared. You're hungry, sure, but hunger is hardly an excuse to ruin such an exquisite and expensive living arrangement.

When you got back from the agency you checked the bedroom, the kitchen and the bathroom, and you certainly weren't disappointed. The bedroom houses a four-poster bed, with luxurious folds of lacy fabric draping from the posts that are the whitest white you can remember seeing. In the kitchen, you found an Italian oven, delicate crockery, and complimentary chocolates, which you ate already. The backsplash is sleek and the refrigerator has a water dispenser. But it was in the bathroom where you the found the crown jewel of this luxury habitat—a Jacuzzi. Your head filled with scenes of you nestled in a fragrant mess of bubbles, your hair piled on top of your head and a flute filled with spiked lemonade in your hand. A seaweed face mask, too, and maybe even a burning candle. After looking at your new apartment, you were completely satisfied with its potential to provide indulgent isolation, an isolation filled with overpriced sashimi and one deprived of human molestation. You need money for such an indulgence though, you know that, and sooner or later your bank account will be licked clean of its contents. But you don't bother loitering on such irrelevant details for the moment.

In bed, you pretend you are wearing a silk nightgown rather than your dirty ensemble that you have worn for three days straight. The hotel receptionist's coat is still hanging in the closet by its lonesome. The smell of fresh linen is a smell that you had forgotten long ago, and the softness of the sheets almost convinces you that you're Cleopatra. You could get used to this. The best part is you don't even know the name of the street you're on; you neglected to pay attention to it on the paperwork. As you drift to sleep, you wonder how many missed calls you have from Winnie and Alejandro, and you find yourself hoping that there are none, that you have been forgotten by them just as the smell of clean linen had been forgotten by you.

❧   ❧   ❧

The next morning you wake up to the sunshine spilling into your bedroom, the light painting a smile on your weary face. Despite the oodles of happiness in the sun's rays, your stomach still has not been fed and it hates you. You decide to go to Starbucks, because surely in America one can never be too far away from Starbucks. You hop out of bed, run your fingers through your knotty hair, and splash your face with water. Before leaving, you put on the stolen coat and pull it tight around your starved body.

It takes you only seven minutes to stumble across a Starbucks, and the victory feeds your confidence. You don't need someone like Cille filling your inbox with file upon useless file to give yourself a sense of direction in life; your seven-minute discovery proves that you can find your way all by yourself. You join the queue of personal assistants who are relying on the quick service here to keep their jobs, all of them eyeing their watches as they count down the seconds until their bosses need to be sipping on sweetened cappuccinos. When you get to the front, you order an iced latte and the lady at the register asks for your name.

You gag on fear.

The lady asks if you're okay. Of course you're not okay, you're never okay. What were you thinking, going to a place that makes money from calling out names? You step away from the counter and leave the shop. Your stomach implores you to turn back around, but you don't listen. Instead, you keep your gaze trained on the footpath, the pink hair glowing in front of your eyes.

But hold on a minute—how can you possibly be blending into the thrum of the city with that audacious pink hair? You probably stick out like a sore thumb. Even if you give your name to no one, you would still be known as The Girl with the Pink Hair. You shouldn't draw this much attention to yourself, you know, it will do you nothing but harm. To hell with personality, you should be dressing with common sense, not with character. You stop in the middle of the footpath, pull out your phone, and Google the closest hairdresser. There is one three blocks away. Perfect.

When you enter the salon, you are slapped with stares, some of which are intended to be hidden but are unsuccessful. A woman with a strawberry blonde bob and matching lipstick greets you, and asks if you have an appointment. "No," you tell her, "it's sort of an emergency."

"What do you need done?" You can tell by the way she looks at your hair with disappointment that she already knows the answer to her own question.

"Just color. And maybe a slight trim."

"What color are we thinking?"

"Black, actually. Jet black."

⚜   ⚜   ⚜

You leave the salon feeling like a whole new woman. In replacement of your waves of cotton candy, you now have a thick, straight helmet of ebony hair that flicks outwards just above your shoulders. All you need now are some chunky gold sleepers and a black turtleneck. The new hairdo encourages you to look up as you walk along the footpath rather than looking down, and you almost forget that your tacky espadrilles are beginning to hurt your feet. You need a new pair of shoes, too, you decide.

As if the streets are listening to your thoughts, you find yourself standing in front of a department store, and you can't be more relieved. You walk into the bustling shop, packed with people desperate to spend money before going back to work. After wandering around the racks of clothes for an hour or so, you have a plastic shopping bag filled with black turtlenecks, gingham cigarette pants, different pairs of gold hoops that vary in size, and a velvet black pair of pointed ballerina flats. As you're about to leave, a thought occurs to you: what about coffee? Not for right now, but in the future. You most definitely are not going to be providing your name to any Starbucks baristas, and you don't have the time to become a "local" at a coffee shop so they don't have to ask your name. You must make your own coffee, in a venal, elaborate way.

You head back into the busy shop and make your way to the kitchen department, where you find the coffee machine section. You find a red retro-style espresso maker that looks relatively simple to use and you lug the box off the shelf—wait!—it's six hundred and sixty-three dollars. Six hundred and sixty-three. There is no way in hell you can possibly afford that with the rest of Alejandro's precious money. Remember, you're useless. But as you go to put it back down, your stomach moans and wriggles about in a snakelike, hungry frustration. A coffee machine really would benefit you and your hunger. Just imagine: a coffee every morning and every night, without ever having to leave the apartment. You look down at your shopping bag hanging from your arm. It's quite a big bag and your purchases certainly don't fill it all up. A box the size of a coffee machine could fit inside. You pick up the box, open the bag, and drop it in.

Done.

On your way out, you cross through the beauty department, and in the corner of your eye, you catch a glimpse of a gorgeous wine-colored lipstick. You could do with a lipstick like that. You pick it up, swipe a swatch onto your wrist, and, satisfied with its matte finish, smoothly drop it into your bag.

You can pick up a bargain better than Winnie.

Impressive.

☙ ❧ ☙

Back in your apartment you change into your brand-new outfit and gaze at yourself contently in the full-length mirror. All you need now is a soft grey cat slinking around your ankles and a dainty tattoo behind your right ear and then you might be able to find yourself on a Pinterest board. The fact that your lips are coated in stolen pigment doesn't detract from the daring magnificence of it; in fact, it's more liberating, more invigorating to know that it took skill to earn that wine hue, not money.

You remove your coffee machine out of its packaging and take it to the kitchen where you find it a snug spot on the counter between the toaster and the blender. You take the instructions booklet and sprawl yourself on the leather couch, and you skim over it for five minutes before deciding that the longer you read the instructions, the longer your stomach will be without coffee. But when you plug in the cord of the machine and press the start button, a thought occurs to you that is rather bothersome, and if it weren't for your freshly blow-dried hairdo, you would have been inclined to rip every single strand of your hair out.

The thing is, you don't have any coffee.

Instead of pulling your hair out you decide to yell at the coffee machine, it's complexion sprayed with tiny flecks of your spit and reddening even further in embarrassment. How can you be so daft as to forget coffee? You really are just as air-headed as Winnie; denying that would be too stupendous of a lie.

In the machine's shiny surface, you catch a glimpse of your reflection, and you freeze. You must be going insane. Screaming at an inanimate object like that, it's plain insanity. Whatever it is, it must stop. It doesn't matter that no one is here to see this episode of yours; the least you can do is act civilized in front of yourself. It's only acceptable to be irrational when you're not watching yourself. So, pull yourself together, or else your hair will frizz and that blow-dry will go to waste. Rational people would duck down to the corner store and buy some grond coffee, and they'd have a hot coffee in front of them within ten minutes. But are there even corner stores in New York? You haven't a clue. Okay, so compromise. Have a look in the pantry, in the cupboards, see if the real estate agency left anything else besides the chocolate. You open drawers and stand on your tiptoes to peer at shelves, but you have no luck. Hold on—but what's this here in the bottom cabinet, next to the waffle maker?

It's a coffee machine.

In fact, it's the exact same coffee machine that you lifted from the store. To hell with rationality. You shriek at every single kitchen appliance you can find.

⚜   ⚜   ⚜

You need to eat. What good is an authentic Persian rug if you die of starvation? And it can't just be a thirty cent can of beans or a handful of pick-and-mix lollies, no, it must be a proper meal, one with three courses and accentuated with sips of ginger beer. But you don't want to pay for it yourself, that would just be cruel to your bank account, and after that previous episode that you don't particularly want to speak of ever again, you want to try your hardest to not be cruel to inanimate things. It's a lot more sensible to be cruel to people. So, you need someone that will pay you. You hardly want to go wandering up and down the hallways of the condo begging for money; they'd throw you right out. You will have to convince someone to pay for you without them noticing you're doing it. Come to think of it, you know exactly the right person to convince. Richmond the Receptionist.

You check your appearance in the mirror before leaving the apartment and heading to the lift. You ask the elevator operator to take you to the lobby and he performs the prestigious task of pressing the button. As you make your way down, you stare at his funny red and gold uniform hat. You'd like to own a hat like that, even if it's just so you can laugh at yourself when you wear it. The elevator *bings* when you get to the bottom and you walk out into the decadent lobby.

Thankfully, Richmond is at reception, trying to make a pen stay upright on the countertop. He only notices you when you're standing right in front of him.

"You play piano?" you ask, gazing at him from underneath your eyelashes.

"I'm sorry, who are you?" For a fleeting moment, you truly believe that you are as insignificant as you'd always hoped to be, but then you realize that he's only ever known you as The Girl with the Pink Hair. You force a smile to hack into your lips.

"I just moved into the apartment that was for rent. Just yesterday, actually." You can tell by the way he looks at you blankly that he's struggling to make the connection, then suddenly, his face lights up.

"Of course! Miss…" Bloody hell, not that question again. You'd really like to stay a stranger for as long as possible. Forever, even. But you can't tell him that you don't have a name. He'd declare you insane and then he'd know that you yell at kettles and saucepans. And so, you tell him,

"My name's Cille."

"Welcome, Cille."

"So, piano?" you remind him. He jeers onto the balls of his feet at the reminder.

"I can play a song or two, actually. My mother used to play for my family on special occasions." His general American accent really is a let-down, but this talk of piano playing is good news.

"Why'd you ask?"

"Well, you see, my apartment has this lovely grand piano sitting in the corner of the living room, but the only use it has is collecting dust, because I haven't a clue how to play it."

"So, you want me to teach you?" You hadn't considered that before, but that's probably because teaching would only mean more talking, and talking is certainly something that you'd like to avoid.

"Oh, no, I was just hoping I could find someone to play it for a bit. You know, fill the room with a bit of ambience. Only if you're not working, of course."

"I'm out of work starting at four."

"So, you'll come up and play a song or two for me then?"

"Sure," he shrugs, "don't see why not."

Marvelous.

You're already imagining the piano notes decorating your apartment as you sip on a bottle of the bubbliest of ginger beer.

Two hours later your doorbell rings, and you peep through the tiny eye-hole to find Richmond waiting patiently for the door to open. He hasn't changed out of his impeccable suit. Upon opening the door, he greets you with an awkward half-wave and a smile, and you strain a laugh in return. When he walks into the living room, he takes a moment to take it all in, his gaze crawling back to the view every time it wanders about. You notice him awkwardly remember that he's not alone, and then it's his turn to strain a laugh. All this nervous laughter is reminding you of how good you are at being unsociable, and you can't help but cringe. Next time pay for your own dopey meal, it'll save you from all this unpleasant nonsense of being in the presence of another person. He gestures to the piano and you nod, and he sits on the stool and wriggles his fingers in preparation.

"I have to warn you," he says, "I haven't played in a while." He softly taps a couple of keys, and his big, manly hands look sublime against the black and white rectangles.

You tell him, "That's better than never having played at all."

And then, with a flick of his wrists and a clearing of his throat, he begins. You worry that the throat clear means he's thinking of singing, too, and you worry he'll be awful—what a way to ruin piano music.

But he doesn't sing, just plays, and the sound that fills the apartment is celestial magic. And his hands, oh, his hands, they are simply too good to be true. His eyes are closed and his eyelashes softly kiss the skin underneath his lower eyelids, and you think you can see a smile curving its way through his lips. It even looks genuine.

The piano, you realize, has even convinced you that you are slightly angelic. Who would've thought.

After he finishes the song, Richmond stands up and bows, and you clap hurriedly. Clap clap clap clap clap. You don't want to say anything in fear of slicing through this blessed moment that Richmond has just created, and he doesn't seem to want to, either. He brings down the cover on the keys and gets up from the stool, pulling his sleeves back down to his wrists. He takes a seat at one of the bar stools in the kitchen and you pour him a glass of water. This silence is a silence you have never really experienced before. A silence that is… warm. The wordless scene is making you feel strangely safe, and you don't feel the desire to fill the room with noise like you do in other silences. This silence that Richmond is giving you is reassuring, and you wish human interaction was always like this. He finishes his water and whips the comforting blanket right off your shoulders. "Was that song okay? I messed a few notes up. Sorry about that."

You tell him it was brilliant.

His gaze begins to wander around the kitchen, sweeping across your disastrous coffee machines. You quickly spit out some words before he can mention anything about them.

"You hungry?"

"Yes, now that I come to think of it."

"We can order takeout, if you want. What sorta cuisine are you into?"

"Oh, no no, I don't want to intrude on your dinner plans." His cheeks go rosy underneath the short stubble, and it reminds you of Alejandro's own cheeks when he invited you to a matinee.

"I don't have any plans. I could use the company." You really couldn't use the company, but he doesn't need to know that. He stares at you for a bit while he considers the offer. You should be careful, because if he stares for too long, then he'll be able to recognize your face if you ever pass him on the street.

"Yeah, okay. I guess I can stay a little while longer."

You end up ordering sushi rolls and miso soup. While you wait for the food, Richmond tries to ask you about your 'origin.' He says,

"So, you're not, like, Western, right? Your skin is too, er, dark." You try desperately not to roll your eyes. You will have none of this small-talk nonsense. You hate small talk because you can never tell whether it's sincere or not. Engaging in it is a waste of your time, and you have managed to avoid it for years now. That was one of the good things about Winnie and Cille—they always got straight to the point, no dilly-dallying on conversation that was designed to go through one ear and out the other. It's times like these when humanity begins to disappoint you, and your patience with it begins to thin. It's like when people won't say how they actually feel. Whenever you make the immense effort to ask someone how they are, they will always reply with "good," no matter what. And it drives you crazy. You want them to burst into tears because they just got dumped, or slap you because they've always felt you were a bitch. You would never do such a thing, though, exposing your true emotions like that, but other people should. You'd prefer it if everyone else was more real. Then maybe you'd give the lady at Starbucks your name.

You keep on giving Richmond one-worded answers

until your doorbell rings. Relieved to have an excuse to stop the conversation, you hurry to the door, but he gets up and hurries right beside you.

"Don't worry, I've got it," he assures.

"Oh, don't be ridiculous, you're a guest here." Look at you, being so polite.

"But," he argues, "I'm also a gentleman."

And there you have it, a three-course meal, all for free.

Step 3

When You See Signs of Being Known, Leave

A WEEK AFTER YOUR dinner with Richmond, you steal a wallet. It was a very spur-of-the-moment decision, and you perspired profusely for hours after the wallet had been swiped from its owner. You cannot deny the fact that you were rather lucky with that catch. But you must admit: you did a pretty good job for someone who is relatively new to this sort of… business. Yes, business, that's a good way to put it. The word business entails professionalism and profit, and you can confidently say that you are in possession of both of those things. You are a businesswoman.

You are now in the presence of four hundred dollars in cash, a membership card for aquatic Pilates, a frequent flyer's card, a debit card, and a photograph of seven Chihuahuas dressed in customized sweaters, each a different color of the rainbow. Of course, the debit card has probably already been canceled by now, but you still have four hundred dollars and a free aquatic Pilates class.

Also, stop feeling so guilty.

This is business.

If people want to be taken seriously by you, then the least they could do is not leave their wallets unattended in booths at diners. Especially the morons who carry around four hundred dollars in cash.

Sitting atop your kitchen counter, the honking hubbub of the choked traffic below floating up and ruffling your hair, you ponder what to spend your earnings on. You'd quite like a few bottles of expensive bubble bath for the Jacuzzi that lathers into luxurious clouds of fragrant suds, but then again, you also wouldn't mind a good-quality silk teddy from Victoria's Secret that you could slip on after spending three hours in the Jacuzzi. Maybe you should spend it all on food, stock the pantry with jars of strawberry jam and bags of microwavable popcorn. But what about headphones? You neglected yours all the way back in Bondi, and by now they are probably jammed into Alejandro's sticky earwax at this very moment. This is proving to be quite the decision to be made. Maybe you should buy a cat, or a fish, and you could ask for its opinion. How much are cats, anyway? Surely no more than four hundred dollars. You could probably use the frequent-flyer points you nicked, too, there's bound to be a couple of hundred on that. But then you'd have to buy cat food, and that would only lead to a furry corpse and a little funeral, because there's no way in hell that you're going to buy cat food. You know what, you should just attend aquatic Pilates before you make any rash decisions.

❦   ❦   ❦

The aquatic center is packed with chlorinated air and too-small speedos, and if it weren't for the fact that you bought a swimsuit on the way here specifically for this occasion, you would turn around and leave right now. At the far side of the center you spot a huddle of fat old ladies, all of them tucking their hair into floral swimming caps and adjusting their mismatched floral bathing suits over their flaps of skin. They're all giggling together. You walk over to the ladies and ask if this is the Pilates class.

"Gawd, no," spits one of them, her gums flapping. "This is aquatic Pilates."

"Meryl!" another one butts in, the woman's swimming cap actually matching her swimsuit, "that's what the poor girl meant, you goose!" Mrs. Matching turns to you and whispers, "don't be frightened by Meryl, she just gets a bit snappy."

A tiny giggle falls from your lips, and you almost jump with surprise. You can't remember the last time you heard a genuine laugh from yourself.

"What are you laughing at, child?" Meryl crows, planting her bony hands on her crooked hips.

"Nothing." And then you giggle a little more. Stop it, goddammit, or else you'll be known as The Giggling Girl amongst the elderly and you'll become a legend that they'll pass down to their grandchildren, and you most certainly do not want that.

"What are you even doin' here, child? Don't you know this class is for professionals?"

"Let her be," soothes Dorothy, the matching lady, laughter twinkling from her eyes, "she can be next to me." She looks up from Meryl and smiles at you, a smile full of warmth and motherhood, and it makes your stomach twist in fear of confronting nostalgia.

"My, uh, my grandma suggested I come here," you mutter quickly.

"And who's your grandma, darlin'?" Your heart rate slightly increases, your pulse softly flirting with the veins within your wrist. Next time you should think before you mutter such nonsense.

"Mrs. June," you finally blurt. Dorothy, whose eyebrows have furrowed into a bushy nest of questions, glances at Meryl, but she just looks plain angry and possibly even willing to accuse you of murder. So, she turns around and pats another one of her friends on the shoulder.

"Patty, darlin', do we happen to know anyone by the name of Mrs. June?"

"She's a librarian," you quickly add. Patty gazes up to the ceiling, and you can tell that her mind is filing through every single face she's ever put a name to, even the ones that she's only ever seen in newspaper articles. Finally, her gaze returns to Dorothy, and she sighs,

"I don't believe we do, I'm afraid."

"Maybe she does the Wednesday night sessions?" offers Dorothy. "Does your grandma do Pilates on Wednesday night?" God, old ladies are too nosy for their own good. They rely upon thick gossip for their survival, and all it does is dig holes behind people and then pushes them right in.

"Probably."

When the instructor finally comes, you are relieved for the excuse to stop talking. The instructor doesn't look much older than you; her hair tied into a ponytail and her legs scrawny and straight. She's wearing board shorts over her swimsuit, and every now and again she puts down her clipboard to pull them back up and over her non-existent hips. The group waddles into the waist-deep pool, the instructor beaming as she barks orders. You quickly strip down to your new black one-piece that has a deep plunge at the back and an even deeper plunge at the front, the leg holes high at the hips. You can already feel the stare of the old ladies burning holes into your smooth, bare skin, the holes deepening as their envy thickens. You gulp. You are easily intimidated. You lower yourself into the pool, where everyone is already hopping methodically from one foot to the other. The instructor yells at the ladies to add arm movements and they do so excitedly, excesses of arm flab flinging through the air and slapping the water. Timidly, you join in, though your movements are sheepish and embarrassing.

"I told you so," screeches Meryl from behind you, "this class is for professionals."

"Do you know someone stole my wallet just yesterday!" There's commotion.

"I was at the diner, and I left it on the table with my coat while I went to the bathroom. I almost had a heart attack when I got back and it wasn't there!" a chorus of gasps sing over the splashing. You thrust your arms back and forth faster. Don't make eye contact. If you make eye contact with any of them, then they'll know it was you.

"Ladies!" yells the instructor, "focus, please! Flapping your gums is not an effective method for conditioning your bodies. Now, into the squats!"

You spend the rest of the class avoiding eye contact and taking criticism about your technique from the old women. Echoing across the center, their voices ping-pong back and forth across your mind, hurting more than the exercises. By the end, you feel nauseous.

You leave the aquatic center before any of the old ladies can grab you by the wrist and drag you into any of their tedious conversations. You pull your coat tight around your body, not bothering to put on the rest of your clothes and just dumping them in your tote, and you swiftly make your way along the sidewalk. Your bare legs attract mounds of unwanted attention in this chilly air, from both by-passers and the icy wind. As you walk along the footpath, face down, pessimism up, your thoughts drift to warmer climates and what, if any, damage your absence has done. Do the people you left behind experience long, restless nights due to the mere thought of you? You want to know if you mean something. It is important for you to know.

But that's the killer, the answers to these questions.

Maybe, you think, maybe that's why you leave every time you are close to a resolution.

You coward.

When you enter the lobby of your condo you are confronted by the inky black splodge of police uniforms. There are three of them in total, one woman with a horridly small bun pinned to the nape of her neck, one man with a crooked hat, and another man who has a voice that vibrates throughout the lobby like Zeus himself. As you walk past the trio on your way to the lift, you notice that Richmond is huddled with them, too, wringing his glorious hands nervously. You strain your ears in an attempt to hear their conversation. Snippets of it float over.

A girl with pink hair.

Bondi. As in Sydney-Australia-Bondi. Cotton-candy pink.

Quickly, get into the lift. Faster! Just press the goddamned button yourself, there's no time to ask the lift operator to do it. You ask him if he can make it go any faster. He shakes his head. Down the corridor, into your apartment. You stand in the middle of the Persian rug and you look out onto your immense view. You think about what you just heard. The broken shards of words slit at you. And then you think, pack your bags. Why? Well, there are several reasons.

Four thousand dollars.

A disappearance, almost like a magic trick.

A coffee-less coffee machine

Accompanied by lipstick the color of red wine.

A coat that smells of dusty linen and expired dreams.

Aquatic Pilates and a family photo of Chihuahuas.

Shove everything into your tote bag, everything. You don't have time to change into something dry, you'll have to make do with the swimsuit and coat for now. Just shove the clothes into the bag. Oh, and grab a book from the bookshelf. Have you got the four hundred dollars? Just grab the whole wallet. You shuffle to the front door, look around for anything you've missed, and—the coffee-less coffee machine and it's duplicate.

If they decide to search your apartment, they'll question the twinning coffee machines, and before you know it, you'll be greeting your new concrete cell. You need to take one with you. So, you shake everything out of your tote and carefully place the stolen coffee machine at the bottom of the bag. You replace everything back in the bag, making sure to cover any glossy vintage red. Upon picking up the lipstick, you make the decision to give your lips a quick coating.

As you place the lid back onto the stick, you hear something that curdles your blood.

A piano note.

And then another one.

Reverberating throughout your mind, it is a soundwave so big that it confuses the imagined with the real.

Ding.

Ding, Ding.

You look over to the empty stool, to the keys as they lower by themselves.

Ding.

The air is so

Ding,

So,

Ding,

Cold.

Block it out.

You open the door, lock it behind you, and step into the plush corridor. Now, remain calm. Or else.

You coolly walk along the corridor, taking your time to observe the paintings on the walls and the flowers in the vases. This is just stupidity, all it's going to do is draw more attention to yourself. When you step into the lift, you choke on your words as they fight each other to roll off your tongue, none of them sure as to whether they want to win or not. Quit choking. Remain bloody calm.

"Lobby?" asks the operator, and you shove your words down your throat and quickly nod. When the doors open, you are staring at a crooked police hat. Smile, quickly. Make your eyes light up with joy, make them twinkle. Richmond, you notice, is standing behind the crooked hat, with the rest of the officers.

"Richmond!" you shrill, as if you were the friendly type.

"Err, Cille, hey." Something flicks within his eyes, maybe disappointment, or guilt. And then you know he knows. You know you are already a villain. But what's extraordinary, is that within this flicker of emotion, you can tell that he wants to help the villain. Because the conflict of doing such a thing, well, it's tangible. You can feel its tendrils, tickling the tip of your nose and making your cheeks flush. You step out of the lift and the trio plus Richmond step in.

"Have a nice day, Cille." His gaze doesn't quite meet yours, possibly in fear of blurting out nonsense about The Girl with the Pink Hair. And as the doors of the lift begin their journey to meet in the middle, you find yourself thinking that, in an alternate universe, you and Richmond could visit orchestras, and each time the conductor bows, you'd tell him that his piano playing is still the best piano playing you've ever heard.

❧ ❧ ❧

The airport is bustling with loads of people making their way, and despite the sticky puddle of paranoia that your brain is swimming in, it comforts you. For now, you are a blank space to them. Before asking the cabbie to drop you at the airport you asked him to take you to a travel agency. You had again planted yourself in front of the list of special offers, flicking through them and all their possibilities. And as much as Cairo seemed adventurous and London seemed aesthetic, your gaze couldn't help but keep flicking back to one particular city, its name demanding your attention even when you put in so much effort to deprive it of your attention. Even just looking at those eight letters makes your head spin with distorted scenes from the perspective of a little girl that you were once able to call 'me,' and you shunned those sickly distortions before they were able to recover and live in your thoughts.

You ended up choosing that city, though, in fear of the letters jumping off the sign and beating you to death. The travel agent, seemingly aware of your attraction to this paradise, knows you are not strong enough to resist its charms, and when you nod affirmatively as in *book my ticket*, she sits with her arms crossed and a look plastered on her face that could only be translated as *I told you so.*

The frequent-flyer card actually had a lot of points, and to pay for the flight you used all of them up in satisfaction. On the plane, you sleep the whole way, the exhaustion of your worrying thoughts getting the better of you. Sleep, after all, is the only break people get from life, and that is perhaps why you do it so often. But in quick moments between sleep, your thoughts keep wandering back to the grand piano. The hollow notes that wafted from it as it stood next to the empty stool.

The notes crescendo in your mind
Ding
As you ponder
Ding
Whether you are
Ding
Ludicrous
Ding
Or not.

Don't be silly. You're not ludicrous, you were just panicking. Your adrenaline dramatized the event, is all, feeding off the police uniforms and hushed whispers.

At least you can blend in now though, with your black hair just as black as the blackest of souls. But you're still wearing your swimsuit and stolen coat, giving you a disheveled appearance that only serves to gain unwanted attention. Once the plane touches down and you're in the airport, you scurry to the bathroom and change into your turtleneck and cigarette pants. You even apply another coat of that wine-colored lipstick. It looks good on you, you know. You stuff the cozzie and coat into your tote bag and head to the exit. Someone tries to put a ridiculous lei around your neck but you shoo her away and proceed. As soon as you step foot out of the airport, you regret your choice of apparel; your skin swelters under the thick fabric as dense waves of heat slap your rosy cheeks. In fact, you regret coming here in the first place. Because the only thing more unpleasant than the heatwaves in this city are the memories you once made amongst them.

❧   ❧   ❧

Honolulu once broke your heart. Or rather, Honolulu housed the event that broke your heart. Same difference. The point is, you once promised yourself that you'd never come back. Yet here you are.

Moron.

You shouldn't have taken Cille's money. Nor the stupid coffee machine. You can't keep lugging it around with you. It's hurting your arm. And you don't have anywhere to stay, not with four hundred dollars and a tacky collection of earrings. Well, there is one place. But you couldn't go there. *Shouldn't* go there. Much to your disgust, you can picture that house in your mind as if you had just left it the day before. It's big front yard decorated with potted plants and not enough grey pebbles, the angel statue made of marble that spurts water from its mouth, and the doormat that says *Aloha* in blue cursive. You can picture your older sister, Naomi, rocking softly in the hammock on the front porch with a book in her hand, her brown waves of hair tumbling over her chest. You can even see her dimples, the ones that used to appear when you sang together in the kitchen and you got the lyrics all mixed up. You can picture the house's great big windows that welcomed in buckets of sunshine and soaked the place with comfort. And the scent, the scent of jasmine that permeated the walls and wafted through the doors, you can smell it right now, flirting with the blurry recollections of childhood. Your mum had planted that jasmine, hadn't she?

Sepia memories of your mother infiltrate the crevices of your soggy, pink brain.

Stop thinking.

Make a plan, quickly.

Either go to the house or not, but quit pondering and make a decision. You cannot stand in this airport forever—the tourists that opted for a lei will see you without one, assume you're a local, and will be asking you for directions soon enough, even though they could just ask the driver of their minivan. So, house or hotel? Considering your financial position, you're better off choosing the house. Goddammit, you hope Naomi isn't there.

You hail a cab and give the house's address to the driver. Driving through Waikiki sends a wave of reminiscent dread down your spine, and you can't help but kick yourself. What if you bump into someone you know? Sure, everyone here only remembers you as a brunette, with thick, luxuriant waves of hair just like Naomi's, but despite your jet-black bob you're probably still recognizable. Should've gone blonde. Now you can really feel the sweat coming on, and you have to pull at the neck of your top to achieve some decent airflow. Should've stayed in your swimsuit. Looking out the window, the scenery seems to be undeterred by your frustration, and is presenting itself in a dazzling manner that is hard to ignore. The skies are bluer than your mood, free of clouds and blemishes. The palm fronds that hang high from the trees create lacy patterns of green against the line where the sky meets the town, and the route is full of pretty little houses that look like they're bound to have organic honey in their pantries. You wish you were the only one in this exuberant town, and then every single pot of organic honey would be yours, and you could share them with the palm trees and the wild chickens that cluck their way along the side of the road. You wish you were the only one in the whole universe.

Amid your daydreams, the driver stops. It appears that you have reached your destination. You scurry out and pay with a bit of the four hundred dollars that came with the old lady's wallet, and then station yourself at the front gate. The house looks exactly how you left it three years ago; it's as if you never left at all. Vines of jasmine are meandering across the gate and the grass is the green of crisp dollar bills. The big pots of lavender are luxurious and the hibiscus bushes are lavish with big red flowers. Even the frangipani trees are flowering. The house's white exterior isn't any less white than it was three years ago, and the tremendous windows are welcoming you in. And look, even the hammock is still there! It's swaying ever so gently. Oh, God. Now that you pay more attention, there is a rippled curtain of brown hair draped over the edge of the orange fabric.

You can turn around right now if you want. Just make sure she doesn't see you.

A leg flops out of the hammock, a bare foot landing on the floorboards of the porch. Please don't get up. Another foot plods onto the floorboards. She's going to get up. Stay or run. Quickly, decide. She's standing now, tying her hair up into a bun on top of her head. God, did you glue your feet to the ground or something? *Move!*

Too late. She's seen you.

And she does not look happy.

Naomi steps off the porch and walks over to the gate, arms crossed and forehead corrugated. Surprisingly, you feel your stomach drop a little, as if you were hoping she'd be happy to see you. She stops a couple of feet away from you.

"What are you doing here?" Even with the hostility of the question, her voice is still as sweet as the jasmine.

"Just wanted to swing by, is all." Your words are laughable—psychotic, even—after what's gone on. You can't seem to make eye contact with Naomi, not yet.

Naomi is the crier of the family; you are the nightmare of the family.

Naomi opens the gate and turns to the house, silently letting you know you're allowed in, and you follow her. In the middle of the yard, she stops and turns around to you. She stares at you a little, curious and judgmental. This intense scrutiny, the intimacy of that gaze, is the closest to home you've felt in three years—but it's also why you avoided it for three years.

You follow Naomi into the living room, passing the *Aloha* doormat, and you take a seat on the couch and wait for her to fix you both a tall glass of iced tea. After a couple of minutes, she joins you on the cream couch, both of you cradling a cold glass of peach tea, home-brewed, according to her.

"I've got something for you," you tell her, dunking your hand into your tote. You pull out the coffee machine, most of the bag's contents spilling out in the process.

"Here you go." You place the machine between the both of you on the couch. Naomi picks it up and drops it in her lap, admiring the glossy red surface.

"I don't really drink coffee anymore."

"Oh."

"At least it's pretty; it will look good in the kitchen." An awkward silence wedges itself in between you and your sister, and all you can manage to do amongst it is take little sips of your tea. Finally, Naomi speaks up.

"How come you brought such a big coat to Hawaii?" You look up from the ice cubes floating in the tea to see that she's staring at the hotel man's coat, which is sprawled on the waxed floorboards along with the rest of your belongings.

"I guess I left in sort of a hurry."

"Seems like a funny thing to quickly pick up in the middle of Summer in Australia." Her comments are blunt and aggressive. Too rough to touch.

"Yeah. I guess."

A little bit more silence.

"So how was your flight? Isn't it, like, ten hours from Australia or something?"

"Ten hours from New Zealand."

A little more silence, curdling any hope for reconciliation.

"You'll stay here?"

You could cry.

Naomi continues drinking her tea while you go to prepare your bedroom. You're nervous to see what it looks like after three years. You're scared it'll look exactly the same, and it'll trick you into thinking you'd never left. That could be a plausible cause of insanity, you know. Even sitting here on the couch, your gaze wandering over framed photos and canvases of art, it's as if you are still sixteen years old.

"Don't throw anything out!" Naomi calls from down the hallway.

Naomi is more of a mother than a sister. From the age of seven she knew how to work the washing machine, took pride in baking cupcakes for you, knew which tea to brew for each ailment. It's almost as if God knew you'd need more than one mum. It's a pity she looks so much like your proper one, meandering brown hair to the waist, thick and familiar cappuccino skin and espresso eyes. Every time she smiles it blooms like a fresh flower. If she didn't look so much like your mother, maybe you'd hang around her a little more often. Maybe you'd want to be a sister, rather than this estranged version of daughter-orphan.

The room, as you had anticipated, is just how you left it. There's still your lacy white duvet on your single bed that you got for your eleventh birthday, and posters of Bruno Mars and Shakira fill the majority of the wall space. And there's your vanity, with its oval mirror and stubborn drawers. The fairy lights are still pinned around the window, and there's still a dark grey smudge on the bedpost from where your mother once scuffed out her cigarette. You want to throw everything out.

You return to the living room, where Naomi is in the middle of taking empty glasses to the kitchen.

"If I could borrow a couple of clothes," you say, "that would be good. Just for a day or two, until I get my own. I only brought warm clothes."

"Fine. I'll see what I have." After she takes one more look up and down you, Naomi says "It feels… good to see you."

You feel terrible.

   ✿ ✿ ✿

You end up waking from your nap at dinnertime, an aroma that isn't unfamiliar wafting from the kitchen down the hallway. You didn't actually need that nap, really; you never get much jetlag of any sort. And anyway—you're used to full days of sleep and full days without. You roll out of bed and amble out to the kitchen, where Naomi is stirring the contents of a crock pot, the features on her face stern and somehow distant.

"Whatcha making?" you ask, peering into the pot.

"Mum's chili, do you remember?"

Yes, you remember. How could you not? In fact, you remember it so well that you can see the three of you sitting at the small round dining table, spooning your mother's delectable concoction onto your plates and giggling as your noses run from the chilli's strength. It's pathetic of Naomi to try and recreate something as pure and long ago as that, absolutely pathetic.

"I don't want any," you say.

Naomi shakes her head.

"But I made this especially for you. I didn't make this for me. You've got to get over yourself and cooperate if you're staying here." You watch her as she sucks in deep breaths, her baby hairs sticking out in wisps from her temples.

"I'm just not that hungry," you say. As you walk back to your room, your stomach does its "hating you" growl.

You can hear Naomi curse under her breath. Her pain is a poisonous gas that you can't help but breathe in.

❧   ❧   ❧

Two hours later, there's a soft knock at your door. Instead of saying anything, you continue to lie on your bed in the darkness staring intently at Shakira's mane of hair. Maybe you should consider that look for yourself, even the *Laundry Service* tattoo. Another soft knock, this time longer. When you still don't show any sign of responding, the door is opened and footsteps pad over towards you; then the side of your bed dips down with the weight of a person. The sweet smell of Naomi's coconut moisturizer surrounds you and calms you down.

"I'm sorry." Her voice is even sweeter than her moisturizer. "This has kicked up a lot of memories." Stupid her, if only she knew you've managed to not have memories for almost three years. "I wish I was prepared to deal with you, like a good sister." She's wasting her breath, her speech as futile as her dinner plans. You just want her to shut up and leave, so that you can be consumed by the darkness and rid of your sad flashbacks.

"But I can hardly stand to look at you," she adds. You wish Bruno would leap off the walls and shoo her away. "Anyway, um, I put some clothes on your vanity for you."

She sniffles and tells you sorry again.

And with that, Naomi stands up and leaves you with the almighty darkness and your self-conception. Naomi's pessimism is entertaining, at least.

Step 4

Deactivate
Your Electronic Self

THE NEXT FEW WEEKS are spent tasting every flavor of shave ice and eyeing down men who row outrigger canoes as you lie on the fabulous beach. You borrow books from Naomi and read them in the hammock while sucking on lemon sherbets, and you fill your wardrobe with a collection of new outfits and guises. You stay out of Naomi's way and she stays out of yours. You avoid cafés and create new recipes at home, ranging from raspberry ice lollies to zucchini noodles. You even manage to make a few coffees with the red coffee machine. So far, you haven't bumped into anyone who recognizes you, and you plan on maintaining that status. You are bored, yes, but you don't really mind. As long as you don't deteriorate, you are fine. You can endure this monotony just like you can endure yourself. You are lonely. You are light-headed. You can never decide whether to cry, or scream, or sit very still for an hour or two. At least your ice lollies are delicious. Naomi keeps pestering you to get a job, or else you'll have to stop using her things, but you know for a fact that she won't actually enforce such a condition, even if she despises you—she'd feel too guilty.

Today, while you're putting a book back on the bookshelf, three books from the highest shelf tumble to the floor with a thud.

"Don't scuff the floorboards!" calls Naomi from the bathroom. You pick the books up and replace them on their shelf. As you turn your back to the books, you hear another loud thud. Two more books have fallen. "Would you quit it!" yells Naomi. You put the books back. And you stand in front of them, watching. Nothing moves. *Don't you dare start going insane*, you silently plead. You begin to walk away.

Thud.

Yet another book is sprawled on the floorboards. Naomi stomps out from the bathroom and into the living room, thick with frustration. "How hard is it to keep the books on the shelf?" She bends down and picks the book up, and hurriedly stuffs it back into its slot. She huffs, blows on her freshly painted fingernails, and turns on her heel.

THUD.

Naomi turns back around. You stare at the newly fallen book with a fond curiosity.

"Am I causing this?"

She throws you a scowl and groans, "Don't be so ridiculous."

THUD.

"There's probably just a draft. Check that all the windows are closed. Go." You scurry off and do as you're told. All the windows are fastened shut.

"There's no draft," you tell her.

THUD.

Naomi is so startled that she can't seem to say much. You look to her as you wait for an explanation. She's the one that's lived here her whole life, after all.

"Maybe," she finally breathes, "maybe it's Mum. Maybe she's come to say hello. Even give you some book recommendations."

Her lips curl into a smirk as her gaze fixes itself on the bookshelf.

"I'm just kidding, idiot," she spits, "I'm calling a handyman. It's probably just a loose shelf."

This whole thing is just outrageous, and you'd be in your right mind to simply go to bed and let sleep take care of things. In fact, you'll do just that. You strut to your room and lock the door behind you. You don't want to risk the chance of insanity creeping into your room to join you in your sleep.

❧   ❧   ❧

"I'm going out!" calls Naomi as she fumbles with her

house keys and shoves her feet into a pair of block heels. You walk down the hallway to the front of the house to see her off.

"When will you be back?"

"Whenever I get back!" she shrills. "There's heaps to eat in the kitchen."

Her voice fades as she steps out into the balmy night air. Once she closes the front door behind her, you lock it and head to the kitchen.

After spending several minutes staring at the fridge and refraining from opening it, you decide that you could do with a little outing, too. You pull on a pair of distressed denim cut-offs and a crop top and you slick your hair back into a stubby ponytail at the nape of your neck. You shove the spare house keys into your front pocket, step into a pair of flip-flops, and head out to the yard and onto the street. You walk until you get to the middle of Waikiki, the sound of laughter and optimism filling the warm navy air.

The Honolulu Cookie Company is a franchise that remains the best part of your childhood. It never ceased to amaze you how many shops they had dotted around Hawaii, filled with pineapple-shaped biscuits that melted on your tongue and sent you into a state of dopey euphoria. Oh, and the free samples! Every time you entered one of their shops, you would pick one sample of every single flavor, and you'd thoughtfully crunch on each one, with Solomon-like consideration. Your favorite flavor was dark chocolate and coconut.

You think that if you were eaten, you would taste like that, too.

Perhaps you should feed yourself to the devil.

Walking into one of the shops now is like walking into a warm, sugary hug. The shelves are filled with an innumerable amount of cookies, each and every single one shaped and packaged identically. And there's the sample containers, waiting for you to take a rare trip down memory lane. You pick out a little square of biscuit from each container, sixteen in total. You start with triple-chocolate macadamia. It is exquisite, a gastronomic masterpiece that could be too delectable for most civilians. Then you move on to the guava—Naomi's favorite, if you recall correctly. You can remember her eyes growing with glee every time the two of you entered the Honolulu Cookie Company, arms linked and tongues swimming in saliva. Yes, guava was her favorite. She liked how the shortbread in it was tinged pink. You nibble through your samples, ending with a white chocolate kona coffee, and decide that this is the most fun you've had in a while. Winnie would've enjoyed this, come to think of it, and Cille.

You take six triple-chocolate macadamia cookies and two guava ones to the front counter, along with a hibiscus-shaped cookie tin from the array of unique tins on the shelves. As the girl behind the counter packs your cookies into the tin, you can feel her gaze assessing you with an utmost curiosity. You pretend to be particularly fond of the pamphlets on the counter advertising their special edition Valentine's Day cookies. Before slotting the last cookie into the tin, the girl asks, rather loudly,

"Do I know you?"

You look up from the pamphlets and quickly scan her face, making sure to not give her too much of an opportunity to get a decent look at your eyes. Now that you're paying more attention, you realize that her face looks familiar to you, too. She went to middle school with you, didn't she? As if reading your mind, she continues, "Didn't we go to middle school together? Kaimuki Middle School?"

Dammit, you screech silently, *I went to Kaimuki Middle School.*

"You must be thinking of the wrong person," you quickly assure her.

"Maybe it was elementary school?"

"I'm actually from Australia. Born and raised there and everything."

"You don't sound very Australian."

God, why does she have to be this stubborn?

"My parents are from Hawaii."

"Ah, I see. I guess you just look a lot like someone I used to know. Sorry about that!"

She pushes the tin across the counter to you and bids you a goodnight. You hope that she doesn't go searching through her yearbooks when she gets home. Get away quickly.

❦ ❦ ❦

When you exit the shop, and turn onto the footpath, you almost run into a parked bike. It's a very nice bike, with a vintage frame and seafoam-blue paint. It even has a basket at the front of the handle bars. You could do with a bike like that. It looks very relaxing to ride, with its big wheels that look as if they are made to cruise effortlessly past little coffee shops and smoothie bars. And whoever owns it clearly doesn't love it that much, for they haven't attached it to anything with a bike lock; it's free to be taken by anyone.

Oh, come on, just swing your foot over it and off you glide.

Yes.

You hitch your leg up and climb onto the brown leather seat. You position your feet on the pedals, and push off.

Congratulations, you now have a brand-new bike.

Never mind, you've got company.

There's a woman running directly towards you, her face squished into anger. She's charging ahead. You're still on the bike, pedaling. Stop pedaling. No, pedal faster.

Oh, bad idea.

You're flying through the air.

The woman is tumbling with the bike, her foot jammed into the spokes of the front wheel, her hair tangled into the basket. You're still flying, the footpath your destination. You brace for a face plant. Or maybe you'll just keep flying whilst the woman keeps rolling and—your face is numb.

Pressed onto the sidewalk, you hear the woman stomp towards you, and her spit lands into your ear. She finishes off her rage by planting a kick in your ribs.

More spit. Angry huffs. You are called a bitch.

You unfurl yourself, wheezing. Get onto your feet. Slowly, licking blood from the side of your lip, you walk away. Some people.

        🐝   🐝   🐝

At two in the morning, you hear the front door unlatch and heavy footsteps pad across the floorboards. For a few sharp seconds you panic, completely convinced that the owner of the bike is in your sister's house baring a jack-knife and a mallet, ready to pounce on you as soon as you so much as whimper. But then, to some disappointment, you remember that Naomi lives here, too.

She struts to your room and flicks on the light. You squint at her irritably.

The bruises on your temple are throbbing. Oh, God. Here we go again.

"What the hell happened to your face?" she yells. "Where did you go? I never told you to go anywhere!"

You roll your eyes, already sick of her company.

"I didn't go anywhere!" you yell back.

"Then explain the blood."

"I tripped."

"That's rubbish. You tell me who did this. Or else once I found out myself, I'll throw you out."

Naomi proceeds to stomp down the hallway, muttering, her heels click-clacking on the floor. You follow her.

"I tripped," you tell her again, taking in the strap of her camisole that had fallen off her shoulder and her lips that sparsely wear the remains of a loud lipstick.

"How did you trip?" she challenges, her voice lacking its signature sweetness.

"None of your business."

"Don't give me that crap."

"Who cares how I tripped, okay? I fell and that's that."

You drag yourself back to your room and into bed, pull the blankets over your shoulders and turn your back to the door, stamping an end to your side of the argument.

You feel Naomi's gaze bore into your back, in between your shoulder blades. She could be mean if she really wanted to, she could be truly mean, but not to you. As your older sister, she has one of those obligations to you that is never spoken out loud, but is just known. Especially after your mother died, she would never forgive herself if she properly hated you. That's why her voice is always sweeter than anything. Sometimes you feel sorry for her, though, because it's not her fault that she had to become your mother as well as your sister—after all, it's a lot to ask of a twenty-year-old who had just lost her mother, too. She must be spiteful, though. Who wouldn't be if the only family they had left on this world was you?

"By the way," you murmur, only just audible, "I got you cookies. Guava ones."

You idiot, no you didn't.

You left the cookies scattered on the sidewalk.

❧ ❧ ❧

Three days later, after eating two frosted blueberry Pop Tarts for breakfast and completing the Sudoku in the local newspaper, you propose an idea to Naomi, one that took you no longer than four and a half minutes to concoct—that's eight bites, if you're measuring according to your breakfast.

"Naomi," you call out to the house, "I have a suggestion."

Naomi scuttles from the depths of the house to the kitchen, where she pulls out a bar stool and tentatively sits herself on top.

"Continue."

"I was thinking, you're a very busy woman, and you work very hard day-in, day-out at God knows what, and so I reckon, you should go on a vacation, just for yourself, a nice break for a couple of weeks."

"Are you trying to kick me out of my own house or something?"

You roll your eyes. "Is it so bad for me to appreciate you?"

"You can't even remember what I *do* for a living! Where do you expect me to go, huh? I don't have that much money to spare, you know."

"I was just about to get to that, before you interrupted

me." You clasp your hands together and clear your throat. "I rent an apartment right in the middle of New York City. You can go there, and then you won't have to pay for accommodation."

Naomi finds herself looking bewildered. "You rent an apartment in New York City? You?"

Her lack of faith is almost heart-breaking, but not quite.

"Yep," you confirm, "with a view and everything. The receptionist is nice, too."

You take your phone out of your pocket and pull up photos of the condo and its location on the map, Naomi's mouth agape as she stares at the screen with intent admiration.

Who's the impressive one now?

Not Cille and her knowledge of herbs.

Not Winnie and her marble kitchen tops.

Not even Alejandro, with his thick Spanish accent and circle of tough guys.

It's you.

You tell Naomi it's all hers.

You tell her that you both need a break from each other. That your pain is too intense, too fresh, and you're sorry for barging in like you did, but you just wanted to be home again. Clearly having you both here isn't working. That she ought to treat it as an emotional cleansing. Just go there for a bit of sanity.

After a couple more hours of conversation that consisted mostly of doubt on Naomi's part and persistent reassurance on yours, your sister finally gives in to your plan. You help her book a flight, assuring her that a one-way ticket would be a grand choice, as it made for excellent flexibility and added a spontaneous fling to the whole adventure which you promise would make her more alluring. Trust me, you had told her, combine a one-way ticket to New York and a moisturizing hair mask and you'll be the most mesmerizing girl in town. Not that you speak from experience, but she doesn't need to know that.

"One more thing," you tell her once the tickets are booked, "If anyone asks who you are, don't mention me."

"Why, what did you do?"

"I didn't do anything."

"Then why can't I mention you?"

Too. Many. Questions.

"Naomi, just trust me, please. Just say you're a friend of a friend of a friend, and that you don't even know my name."

"That's the most untrustworthy thing I've ever heard."

"Ah, have a little faith in me."

    ⚭ ⚭ ⚭

After dropping Naomi off at the airport and entering your empty home, you feel a weight gently slide off your shoulders, and you close your eyes, feeling lighter than your wallet. Bliss, is what this is, pure bliss. In fact, this is so blissful that it calls for a celebration. Dinner, perhaps, at a restaurant with an expansive menu and drinks with tall straws. It doesn't necessarily have to be expensive, but pricey enough that it requires you to reserve a table. You run through a list of restaurants in your head, pondering the perfect place to reward yourself. Finally, you decide upon The Cheesecake Factory; a classic that is incapable of disappointing, quite unlike yourself. You book a table for one.

In Naomi's room, you ransack her closet for a decent outfit. Most of her clothes are just like the ones she lent you—small and colorful and threadbare. Anybody could look at her collection of clothes and know straight away that she's an islander through and through. She's grounded like that. Eventually you find a black ribbed mini dress with rose applique down the side that you don't mind, and you slip it on along with your velvet ballet flats and gold hoops from New York. You sort through what's left behind of Naomi's makeup collection, browsing through an arrangement of pallets and pencils, applying powders and creams to your features along the way. Just as you are about to close the drawer, your eye catches the flash of a red lipstick the exact same shade of the roses along your rib cage, and you apply it onto a satisfied smirk. After giving your hair a quick spritz of dry shampoo and assessing the final results in the mirror, you applaud yourself.

You look divine, my darling, absolutely dazzling. And to think that anyone ever doubted you!

❧   ❧   ❧

At The Cheesecake Factory, you are shown to your seat and fixed with a menu and a tall glass of mineral water. After perusing the menu for a lengthy period of time, pausing every now and again to purse your lips at a funny flavor combination, you order a dish called Pasta Da Vinci, because you love *The Da Vinci Code*, hoping that if it doesn't taste good then you can tell them that and they won't make you pay. You also order a side of buffalo wings, an Oreo milkshake, and a bourbon and honey martini, just to make sure your dinner is well rounded. When you order the martini, the waiter frowns.

"I'm sorry, ma'am, but how old are you?"

Does he really think you're under eighteen? You're slightly offended; you think you look rather sophisticated. And then you remember—you're in the United States of America, where the drinking age is twenty-one. You're not going to let something as insignificant as a number ruin your night, though, no siree Bob.

"I'm twenty-one," you tell him, as confident as a twenty-one-year-old who wants her bourbon and honey martini. The waiter, thankfully, takes your word for it, confirms your order, and attends to another table.

Your food arrives and you devour every last morsel with a flourish. To your delight, the Pasta Da Vinci tasted sublime, giving your night a delightful apotheosis. You signal for a waiter to come over, and you ask him to bring over the dessert menu. This is the part you've been looking forward to the most. The selection of cheesecakes overwhelms you with a childish excitement, as if you're once again five years old and about to spend your three dollars and fifty-eight cents to the fullest in a candy store. You keep tossing it up between the Chocolate Tuxedo Cream Cheesecake, the Lemon Raspberry Cream Cheesecake, and the Coffee Cream Chocolate Supreme, and eventually decide upon the latter, because you like how the name rhymes.

When the waiter places the slice of cheesecake in front of you, you feel your phone vibrate in your bag, and you roll your eyes and fish it out. This most certainly is not the time for a phone call. You look at the screen: you have three texts and two missed calls from Alejandro. Again, not the time for a phone call to intrude upon your elegance, let alone a phone call from Alejandro, no matter how delicious his voice might sound coming out of the speaker. You discretely drop the phone next to your feet under the table, and after looking around for any stares or glances, you lift your chair a little and bring one of its legs down onto the screen, hard and fast.

Crack.

You bend down and pick it up, and find your way to the bathroom. You enter a cubicle and lock the door behind you, and you wrap your broken phone with wads of toilet paper. Then you slide the package into the bin next to the toilet, letting it drop down onto a pillow of pads and sodden tampons.

Perfecto.

Now you can eat your Coffee Cream Chocolate Supreme in peace.

You flush the toilet, wash your hands, and head back to your table, adjusting your dress as if you had been to the bathroom for its designated use.

Eating the cake is like eating the clouds in heaven. You ensure that every single crumb is licked off the side of the fork's tines, sticking your tongue into the gaps. You sag down in your chair, stomach and happiness bursting, and you pull out your wallet from your bag. You regret not asking Naomi to leave you with a bit of cash before she left, because this lonesome twenty-dollar bill squashed sadly next to the photograph of Chihuahuas will not suffice.

You should've thought this through.

What made you think you could afford such a fine dinner with twenty dollars and dressed dogs? You better pick up your game. Now, pull on a strand of hair from your head. You hold a thick, black string of hair between your index finger and thumb and you yank it out, freeing the root. You place the stray hair on the cake plate, and you smear it into the last of the cream and icing.

Now slap that smile off your face. In fact, look disgusted.

Turn up your nose.

When a waiter walks past, you signal for him and he scuttles over.

"What can I do for you, ma'am?"

You narrow your eyes and peer at him through the slits of your eyelids.

"There was a hair on my cake," you announce. You point to the hair on your plate, and he bends down and assesses it. "Goodness, I am very sorry about that ma'am. I'll inform the chef immediately."

You look at him as if he just told you that hair makes food taste better. "I am not paying for such an atrocity," you complain, "that would be absolutely ridiculous." You cross your arms and give out a big, loud *humph*.

"But you ate the whole cake, ma'am."

You roll your eyes, clearly offended.

"The hair was at the bottom of the cake! How could I have seen it!" You look shocked. "I'm going to give you a bad review on TripAdvisor and Yelp. Just look at the strand! It's probably infected with glandular fever."

By now the waiter is sweating, his gaze frantically zipping from the strand of hair to your stony face. By the wrinkle on his forehead, you can tell he is trying to remember how to deal with a disgruntled customer, and you watch him contently while you wait for a reply.

"Your dinner tonight is on the house, ma'am," he finally blurts, wiping a couple of beads of sweat from his brow.

"Fine."

"Is there anything else I can help you with?"

"No," you reply curtly.

The waiter begins to turn away but before he has the chance to leave you call,

"Oh, and don't expect a tip."

Food always tastes better when it's free.

❧ ❧ ❧

As you approach your front gate and peer at the porch, the outdoor light is projecting a stretched silhouette across the yard. You strain your eyes, squinting through the darkness, deciphering the dark muffled shape that wasn't there when you left. You open the gate and walk along the grass, being careful to make your steps silent.

A million different thoughts present themselves, making your chest tighten and your breaths hasten. It's a cop, you think. *No, no, it's definitely Naomi.* But couldn't Naomi let herself in? *She's just misplaced her keys.* It's Cille, then. She's tracked you down. *It's Naomi, I'm telling you!* It's a cop, it's definitely a cop.

When you are only a couple of meters away from the porch you stop walking, letting the night make you invisible. You strain your eyes even further, making out a mop of curls and lanky shoulders. See, it's not a cop, a cop would be wearing a hat. But what if it's a cop in disguise? The figure, who seems to be a man, wanders over to the hammock. He plops down, swings his legs up, and rocks gently, the fabric hiding him from your view. You watch it sway, back and forth, back and forth, your breaths setting themselves in time with the rhythm. Then his legs swing back out, and your breaths hiccup. The man stands up and walks back over to the door, bringing up a hand and sweeping it through his curls.

That action is much too familiar for your liking.

You step closer, quieter than the night.

And then everything hits you all too quickly.

A T-shirt so thin you can see the shape of his slender torso.

The curls, oh, the curls.

The calls that attempted to disrupt your cheesecake.

The fragrance of fabric softener you can only describe as Alejandro's Scent.

You take a step back. Alejandro must've heard you, for his head spins around, and all of a sudden, he is looking right at you. Even in the dark his eyes look ethereal, daring you to attempt to look away. He raises his hand, gives a half-wave, and then shoves the rest of it in his pocket. Without warning, you find yourself walking calmly onto the porch until you are standing right in front of him, so close that if you reached out only slightly your fingers would brush against his chest.

"I tried to call you," he breathes, his accent like champagne.

"My phone doesn't work," you say. He pulls his hand back out of his pocket and reaches out, gently pushing your hair off your face.

"Your hair, it's black now." He surveys your whole appearance, taking it all in. "It's nice, black. It was nice when it was pink, too, and brown."

"What are you doing here?" Your voice is firm, but

frays softly around the edges. You look deep into his eyes, past the glint that you know not to trip over this time. Alejandro frowns, and his gaze darts from yours and settles to the ground.

"Winnie is dead."

His accent must be hindering your ability to understand him.

"I'm sorry, what?"

"Winnie is dead. That's it. She's dead."

You are numb.

Numb.

You… you are numb.

Golden mane, whiskey smile.

You can't see anything, can't hear anything.

You're not numb.

Your chest, it hurts, it aches, right where your heart is.

It is agony.

Oh, how it is agony.

"You okay?"

Wait, someone else is here?

Oh, God, Alejandro's still here.

Your heart is heavy, brick in chest, so, so heavy.

But Alejandro is here.

Your heart will have to use a Band-Aid for now.

"I'm fine," you tell him, "I'm fine."

Instead of letting him settle on the couch, you take Alejandro up to the roof, a place you used to find refuge after your mother died and you wanted nothing more than to be alone with the stars. They were the best listeners, the stars, better than any counselor or sister. You both take a seat, the tiles sliding a little underneath your bums. You look up to the galaxies, still sprawled across the navy blanket of sky, just as you left them all those years ago. The tiles are uncomfortable to sit on— you used to bring up cushions—but it doesn't matter, not when you're in a crisis. The air fills with laughter from a couple of doors down, and it makes you feel cold. Alejandro puts an arm around your shoulders. You shrug it off. You don't care if he gets offended. The clicking of loose tiles sounds from next to you, as if someone had sat themselves down there on the roof. Your mind must be playing tricks on you again, convincing your skull that it's haunted. The tiles shuffle a bit, tapping each other lightly, before coming to a stop. You look over to Alejandro, but he didn't seem to notice. Please, don't be insane. There is nobody else here on this roof, you hear?

"Everyone is worried about you, you know," Alejandro says. "They've been asking and asking, but I had no answers." He turns his head so that he's looking at your cheek, and waits for you to explain yourself. When your mouth stays shut, he continues. "You can't just disappear like that. It makes everyone go *loco*."

"Says the person who disappeared for six months without warning."

"I have a very good reason for that," he defends, "but it deals with stuff that I can't tell people about. It was work stuff, though, so it was for a good cause. I just didn't want to lose my job. If I had told you where I was going, I would have lost my job. Then *I* would be the one going *loco*."

"At least tell me what country you were in, now that you're not there?" A weight lifts off your chest as you divert the conversation from you to Alejandro.

"Okay, but you have to promise to not tell anyone."

Prrromeeese.

"I promise."

"I was in Colombia."

You almost feel like laughing your head off. You saw this coming from a mile away.

"I wonder what you could've possibly been doing in Colombia!" Sarcasm drips from your tongue, bubbly and delicious. Alejandro huffs, frustrated.

"You have to come back. Ever since everyone realized you weren't in Bondi anymore, they all panicked. So many people came knocking at your apartment, and I was the one left to explain to them that you had just vanished! Even your aunt came. And that girl who swears in French, you know, that snobby one? After she heard one syllable of my accent she was convinced that I had smuggled you out of the country! And we all tried calling you, but that didn't work, either."

"As I said, my phone stopped working."

"And what about that money I sent you? What happened to that?"

"It was an emergency, Alejandro. It got me out of a rocky situation."

He sighs, disappointed with your answers that he traveled halfway around the world for.

"When Winnie came to the apartment looking for you, she was such a mess." You hold your breath at the mention of Winnie. "She was... how do you say, *frenético*? She cried and cried. She didn't even go to work. It was like you had died!"

A thick, heavy realization drapes over you.

Your disappearance sent her crazy.

It killed her.

Wait, how did she die?

You killed her.

Oh, Winnie, dear, dear Winnie.

"And so, when we both came to the conclusion that she was the last of your friends to see you, seeing as you stayed the night at her house, I got a feeling she was up to something. It was very suspicious—you, staying the night for her to wake up to find you gone. It just didn't sit right with me, you know? So, I had to remove her from the equation, so that I could focus on you without having her as a threat. Do you understand? I was so worried about you."

Time completely and utterly halts.

Your stomach convulses, your hands become clammy.

You cannot believe it.

You look up to the heavens, asking them if they can possibly believe it.

We cannot believe it, they whisper.

You want to scream until your throat bleeds.

The boy with the nice Spanish accent and smooth back removed Winnie from the equation.

This is not ideal.

Step 5

Extinguish Any Threats

YOU LEAD ALEJANDRO OFF the roof and into the living room, where you sit him down on a couch and fix him a plate of food in the kitchen. You asked the stars to wish you luck before you left. While you cut a loaf of bread, you can hear him rummaging through the huge suitcase that he had brought with him, probably looking for his pajamas and toothbrush. Silly him, he doesn't have to go to all that trouble. When you finish cutting the bread, you brush the crumbs off the knife. You slap a couple of squares of cheese onto the bread slices and put them together to create the most mundane sandwich you'd ever laid your eyes on. You pull a plate out of the cabinet and put the sandwich on top, and then with the plate in one hand and the knife in the other, you head over to the living room.

You take a seat next to Alejandro and put the plate and knife on your lap. Whether he's aware of it or not, you don't care. Alejandro still has his nose buried in his suitcase, and you wait patiently until he sits back up. He has his hands cupped together, a nervous smile decorating his lips. And then he unfurls his hands and presents you with a little black velvet drawstring bag. You look at him, smile tightly, and take the bag from his fingertips. You loosen the drawstring and drop the contents into the palm of your hand, being careful to not drop anything on the floor. In your hand is a necklace, with a thin silver chain and a small, circular pendant. In the center of the pendant is a moonstone, rimmed with silver. The milky rock shines at you, as if it were owned by an angel before Alejandro had bought it, making it perfectly impossible for you to look away. Yes, this necklace must be the property of an angel—there is no other explanation to its beauty. You pick up the chain and undo the clasp, holding it around your neck.

"May I?" asks Alejandro, and you quickly nod, your stomach churning with smothered hatred. The necklace is still very, very pretty, though. Alejandro takes the necklace from you and leans forward so that his hands are behind your neck. You bundle your hair in front of your shoulder, and as Alejandro fumbles with the clasp, you grab onto the knife in your lap, clutch onto it with all your might.

And plunge it into his chest.

You can hear the air chuff right out of his throat.

Blood dribbles into your lap and onto the cheese sandwich. Soggy crimson bread. You push Alejandro onto the floorboards so as to not stain the couch.

A stained couch would ruin everything.

❧　❧　❧

Tears ripple your sight as you look at the dead body on the living room floor. It's proving hard to swallow your saliva; it is even harder to inhale much air.

You are a criminal now, you know.

A proper one.

It's official.

Look at Alejandro, look at his empty, limp body.

You did that, you monster.

Look at the blood pooling beneath him, the blood that's supposed to be pumping through his body, keeping him alive.

Now stop looking.

You did this for a very logical, very rational reason. There is no need to feel remorseful. Alejandro didn't regret killing Winnie, so you should not regret killing him.

Also, stop that awful crying.

Crying is of no use to you.

You always thought that murdering someone would feel a lot more…significant. You thought it would make your intestines coil and your chest implode, crushing your heart as if you had thrown it onto a highway in front of a mighty truck. You thought it would blur your vision and sit atop your shoulders, and that this thunderous "it" would accent your every thought, your every breath, for the rest of your remarkable life, tinting roses a red too dark to be recognized as a color. But you don't feel like that. You don't feel significant. In fact, you feel like the most insignificant girl in the world, like a shadow, crawling, dragging yourself along the sidewalk, unnoticed because you're too ugly and too quiet. And you feel empty, so awfully empty, and so you try to suck in more and more air in an attempt to refill your body, but it is no use. Instead you just gag on the saliva drying in your throat.

You wonder if Alejandro felt like this, too.

Oh, just look at his body, his contorted limbs and his absent expression.

Don't you dare look at his absent expression.

But you're a hero now, don't you see?

You did what most people are too afraid to commit to.

And the knife, the knife that is soaked in the last dregs of his accented, felonious life, a life that had the potential to eternally smell of fabric softener and cash. The wretched knife owns that life now. You better wash it off.

You get up off the couch and head over to the kitchen, knife in hand, where you open a cabinet and pull out a bottle of bleach, something which you merely had to hope that Naomi usually stocked. After rummaging through cabinets and drawers, you find a big mixing bowl and fill it with bleach. You dunk the knife in and, with the aid of wads of paper towel, scrub and scrub at the blade until it is cleaner than a priest's Sunday shoes. You rinse it in tap water, dry it off with more paper towel, take it with you to Naomi's car. You drive for fifteen minutes, dump the knife down a sewer grate, then drive back home.

There shall be no more talk of that villainous knife.

          ❧   ❦   ❧

Now you must dispose of the body. You've read enough books to have a general idea of the method you should employ, and you have watched numerous documentaries and movies that have dealt with the same situation. So, really, this should be a simple errand. You look at the clock mounted on the living room wall to see that it is 12:41 a.m., and you calculate that you'd like to be finished by 5:30 a.m., just before the sun rises. Just before the kaleidoscopic sun can see the red jewels of your decisions. You better get started.

Do not let the blood get underneath your fingernails.

Do not whimper.

Do not dawdle, don't even stop for a glass of water.

As if you even deserve a glass of water.

You get down on your knees beside Alejandro. Your hands tremble. Carefully, you adjust him so that he's lying straight and flat on his back, his thin shirt pressed into the pool of his thick blood. The stench suddenly becomes much too present, and you gag. The metallic twinge of the blood is overwhelming. You gently place one hand on his forehead and the other on his chin, being careful not to hurt him.

Hold on.

Hurt him?

He's dead, you idiot, remember?

You are the hero. His death is your breath of fresh air.

You grip on tighter and open his mouth wide, blood dribbling out and staining his white cheeks. His teeth are also dyed a foul crimson, just like your past. You press the heel of the palm of your hand into his top front teeth, swift and forceful, and they drop onto his tongue that is folded at the back of his throat. You repeat this until all that is left is bleeding gums and a big job for the Tooth Fairy, all thirty-two of Alejandro's teeth piled in his mouth. You quickly get up from your kneeling position, hurry over to the kitchen and grab a mortar and pestle, and then resume your position next to the body. You plunge your hand into his mouth and pull out pinches of teeth, collecting them in the mortar. Once all his teeth are out of his mouth, you begin grinding them. You grind until your arm aches and you're left with a light pink paste made of blood, saliva and a slain smile. You stand back up, take the paste to the kitchen, wash it down the sink, feeling sorry for Alejandro's dentist and all the hard work she might've put into his dazzling smile.

Oh, that smile.

The mask of a monster.

Next you find a carving knife in one of the drawers. You bring it over to the body and sit cross-legged beside it. You pick up one of his hands and place it in your lap. *This hand*, you think, *has been places I could never dream of.* This hand has held illegal money, has gripped onto a phone that had your voice pouring out of it, has run down your body and through your hair. This hand once held your very own hand, held it as if the sky would fall if it were to ever let go. This hand in your lap is probably laden with fabric softener and Columbian marching powder, embedded with splinters of broken promises and scraps of untold truths. This hand holds an entire identity within the finite swirls that decorate its fingertips, a unique pattern that holds every single one of the breaths he took, a picture that tells the story of a boy with a Spanish accent and a curly mop of brown hair. You interlock his fingers with your own, and you stay like that, letting his finger prints tattoo themselves onto the top of your hand.

This hand used to hold your heart.

This hand is cold, is limp.

This hand is a deadly curse.

You must amputate it from your past.

You unfurl your fingers, get up and run to the kitchen, retrieve the bread board, set it down on the floorboards and let his hand drop on it neatly. You position it so that the palm is down and the fingers are splayed, and in one decisive swipe of the carving knife, you chop each of his fingers off.

You let go of the knife and it falls beside you with a clatter, scraping at the wax coating on the wood. You pick up a finger, pinkie, it seems, and you begin to peel off the skin. Your blood curdles, but you can't seem to stop, not now, not after you've come all this way. Once you've stripped it of all the skin, piling it onto the bread board, you begin to tear the flesh from the bone, and when you finish you repeat the whole process until all ten fingers are stripped to the bone.

Deep breath in, deep breath out.

Okay. Moving on.

You take the deconstructed fingers to the kitchen, wrap them in Saran wrap, then foil, and put the package in the freezer. You'll attend to them later.

❦   ❦   ❦

Alejandro's skin is purple and waxy, and the color has completely drained from his lips, his lips that had received so many of your kisses. It's almost as if those kisses were for nothing. Kisses are supposed to linger, are supposed to find a home on another's mouth, but right now they seem to have been completely neglected, as if they were nothing, nothing.

Ah, stop kidding yourself. You are nothing.

No, no. *He* is nothing.

What chance did your kisses ever have of being something if they were received by nothing in the first place?

Come on, let's keep things moving.

You change your clothes and take one last look at your little mess before grabbing your wallet and heading out the door and into Naomi's car. The moon is casting a silvery glow on the front yard, reminding you that you're being watched. You hope the moon doesn't inform the sun of your endeavors. You can't bear the thought of the sun looking down on you, abundantly disappointed, not bothering to pour her warm light through the windows of your childhood house any longer. You'd prefer bashful shouts from the moon and honest accusations from the stars, but never disappointment from the sun. That would be like disappointing your very own mother; it makes your head feel woozy and your stomach feel contorted. It occurs to you that the moon must know every one of your secrets, even the ones that you wouldn't dare to let yourself think of. It must take a lot of work soaking up all those secrets, the type of work that's reserved for best friends and wishing wells.

Thank you, moon, you tell him, *thank you for being my friend.*

You drive to the nearest Walmart, every now and again craning your neck to check that the moon's still watching. Inside the store, you grab a trolley and begin wheeling it up and down the aisles. In your trolley, you put twelve boxes of Saran wrap, a large tarp, a box of garbage bags, an axe that is advertised as an "inseparable companion with a sturdy butt," an oversized men's T-shirt, grey jogger shorts, and kilos of cleaning supplies.

You quickly go back to the aisle with Saran wrap and get another two boxes, just in case. At the checkout you pay with cash, and the cashier asks if you're going camping.

"Yes," you tell her, "a whole group of us are going. I've never been camping before so I'm not quite sure what to expect! I suppose we'll do some sort of ritual, to cleanse ourselves. You know, girl things."

"Well, I can assure you, whatever you do, you won't be needing that much Saran wrap."

"Oh, you're probably right. You never know, though. Camping can be messy."

Back at the house, you change into the T-shirt and jogger shorts and you take the tarp into the backyard and you lay it out flat on the grass like a picnic blanket. You dart back into the living room to where Alejandro is laying and, gingerly, you hook your arms under his armpits and heave his back off the floor. After making sure your grip is secure, you drag his body along the floorboards, leaving a vermilion slick of blood, a trail of a melting raspberry ice lolly, all the way into the backyard and onto the tarp. You take the axe out of one of the Walmart bags that you have lined up on the back veranda, and you decide then and there that this axe is the only inseparable companion you'll ever have. The thought makes you feel a bit sick. At least you have an inseparable companion; many people probably go through their lives without encountering even one. The lawn is bathed in the lights from the house that you purposely left on, making the scene look desolate and theatrical.

It's show time, baby.

Gripping onto the handle with both of your sweaty hands, you hoist the blade high above your head. Tears uncontrollably begin to dribble down your cheeks like a broken tap. You ram the blade into Alejandro's left elbow, slicing the lower arm off the upper. Blood spurts out angrily in thick, ugly splashes, spraying onto the top of your thighs. You quickly scramble away from the tarp before spewing acidic bile all over the lawn, your tongue sour, lips yellow. You clutch your stomach and heave, and your salty tears mix with the bitter saliva that is hanging from your chin. You are still clutching onto the axe, onto your inseparable companion, while you heave. When your stomach hurts from hunching over for too long, you go back to the body and, without allowing yourself to think about it for more than half a second, you dismember the upper arm from the shoulder. Now you're kneeling in dense blood, and the bile on your chin drips down and swirls with the scarlet puddle. You gag a bit, scrunch your eyes shut. You're out of breath from the axe swings. Somehow, without even ordering yourself to, you chop off the left foot. Then his left calf. Don't stop to think about it, just keep going. Cut him from your past. You keep on hacking at the body with the axe until you have completely dismembered it and you're elbow-deep in blood. You cry the whole way through, silently, as if tears had suddenly become your default mode, and your eyes are stinging. You finally let go of the axe, your knuckles cracking as they release from the tense grip you've been maintaining. Chopping up a body takes a specific type of depravity. Unfortunately for you, it seems you are currently in possession of this specific depravity, and it makes you, well, utterly intolerable. Not even your inseparable companion can tolerate you now.

In the bathroom, you scrub the blood off your hands, trying to ignore their trembling. There is a ball of panic wedged tight in your esophagus, and as you're rubbing the last of the blood away, you come to the appalling realization that you still have blood caked on your legs. Your mother wouldn't be proud.

You remember when you were eleven years old.

Your mum had pulled you out of school just so you could hang out with her for the day. You were both perched on a stone wall by the beach, watching the Outrigger canoes roll into shore. You were working your way through a watermelon shave ice, the syrup sticky on your chin, and your mum had a cigarette dangling from her lower lip.

"Mummy, do cigarettes taste good?" you asked her, curiously watching plumes of smoke rise from the cigarette's tip.

"No, not a whole lot."

"Then why do people smoke them?"

She took a drag, removed the cigarette from her lips, and held it in front of her pretty brown eyes, considering your question intently.

"I'm not entirely sure, now that I think about it." She brought the cigarette back down to her lips, but before she could take another drag, more words jumped out of her mouth.

"You know what, why don't you have a try? You never know, you might like it!" Your mum took your half-eaten shave ice from your hand and replaced it with her cigarette. "Just stick it between your lips and breathe in, okay?" She took a spoonful of your shave ice and stuck it in her mouth, her gaze frantically following your timid little movements. You did exactly what she instructed: you stuck it in your mouth and breathed in. You began to splutter dry, hacking coughs that curled your tongue and blurred your vision. You dropped the cigarette on the ground in a hurry. Your mum laughed at you, her eyes bright and her teeth shiny with wet. She reached out and smoothed your hair, her big grin settling into a kind, sorry smile.

"Promise me you'll never smoke, okay? It never did me any good and it sure as heck won't treat you any better. I wish I had cut smoking out of my life sooner." You snatched your dessert from her hand and, after scooping a spoonful of ice, said,

"I can assure you, Mummy, that I never want to do that again."

Right now, looking down at your bloody legs, you can tell that your mother is laughing at you, her laughter pouring out of her eyes. You can hear her say, so clearly, "Promise me you'll never kill a man again, okay?"

"I can assure you, Mummy," you say, "that I never want to do that again."

Though this time, there is no dessert to snatch back.
There is nothing sweet.
Just the relief of cutting the smoke out of your life.

    ❧   ❧   ❧

After you've decided that you can scrub at the blood all
you want later, you go back out to the back veranda and
pick up the bags of Saran wrap. A heavy metallic smell
is hanging wet in the air. The tarp is now completely
covered in a layer of blood, some of it seeping into the
grass, and it's scattered with an array of body parts that
are all tinged crimson. It makes your backyard look
apocalyptic, as if you have somehow trapped yourself
inside a dystopia that doesn't have an exit sign. It's
making your breath very, very sparse.

But the show must go on.

You take a box of Saran wrap out of the bag and rip off
a large sheet of plastic, being careful not to crease it. You
lay it out flat on a patch of grass that isn't contaminated
with blood. Then you reach over to the tarp, pick up an
upper arm, and place it in the middle of the cling wrap.
Pulling the plastic taut, you wrap the limb up like a chef
preparing a chicken Kiev. Once the cling wrap is secure
you put the package to the side and begin the whole
process again, this time with a foot. You continue this
until you have a pile of wrapped body parts idly splayed
across the lawn.

Looking around at the bloody tarp and the plastic

limbs, your hands sticky with Alejandro's blood, you laugh. You laugh not because you are amused, but because you are excessively sad, and you're not sure tears would do your sadness justice. Your laughter is vacant and distant and seemingly uncontrollable, and you have to wait a few moments for it to die down. The poignant hatred you have for yourself in this very moment is at the height of its career. It is the CEO of your body. Its office is spacious and its feet rest on the desk.

You hate it.

Hate!

You have been trapped in a sarcophagus for too long and you want out. You do not care anymore, you don't. I hate you. I hate you for hating me. Give me a chair in your office. I hate you.

You get up off the ground and walk over to the Walmart bags where you pull out the box of garbage bags. You take one out of the box and shake it open. Then you bend down and, one by one, pick up the wrapped limbs and drop them into the bag, opening another bag when one fills up. When you're finished you're left with three bulging garbage bags. Setting the bags aside, you pick up a side of the tarp and let the blood dribble into the yard, drowning the grass until it is mulling in puddle of red wine. You fold the tarp up and shove it into a fourth garbage bag, along with your inseparable companion. It appears Walmart lied to you, because evidently, this axe is separable. Maybe you should file a complaint. They might give you a twenty-dollar coupon to pretend like they value criticism. You could spend it on a stationery kit for your new office. You go inside the house, wash your hands thoroughly, and change out of your clothes that are soggy with blood and stomach juices, replacing them with jeans and a tank top. You pick up the Walmart clothes and Naomi's dress that you were wearing earlier when you executed the extinguishing of your ex-boyfriend, and you add them to the bag with the tarp. Finally, you stuff in the ruined bread board. You tie up all four bags, fastening the knots until the joints in your fingers hurt. One by one, you haul a garbage bag over your shoulder and walk it round to the front of the house where you dump it in the trunk of Naomi's car. Sliding into the driver's seat, you open all the windows and start the engine.

You drive to the furthest public dumpsters you know of, listening to the radio blaring full volume to drown your wheezing. Your knuckles are white as you clutch the steering wheel. The breeze whips limp clumps of oily hair to and fro, knotting it into a black bird nest that smells of raw meat. You look at the time on the dashboard; it's 3:47a.m. You chew at your lips.

When you arrive at the dumpster you hop out of the car and pop open the trunk. You lug the garbage bags out and haul them over to the dumpsters. Then, with as much strength as you can muster, you heave the bags up and over the lip of the dumpster. You dust your hands off in satisfaction.

❦   ❦   ❦

Back home, there is one Walmart bag left on the back veranda: the cleaning supplies. You turn the bag upside down and shake it out like a frenzied housewife would, so that the products are all sprawled across the deck. You take a sponge, cloth, and a bottle each of bleach and detergent and carry them to the living room, where you are faced with floorboards adorned with splodges of thick black blood. Somehow, you managed to avoid getting stains on the couch, and you let out a breath of air you didn't realize you were holding. On your hands and knees, you begin to scrub. You douse a cloth with product and you push it back and forth along the floorboards, adding liters and liters of elbow grease. You scrub until you can once again see the reflection of your plain, tired face in the wax. You work your way through the house, following the smear of blood that's left over from the journey you took with Alejandro's body. You're not sure what's worse; looking down at the floorboards to see blisters of blood or your own reflection staring despisingly back at you.

Once the house is clean, you walk around to the side of the house and unwind the garden hose, uncoiling it so that it stretches all the way to the middle of the backyard. You turn the tap on, the sound of the water rushing through the rubber loud and aggressive against the night's delicate silence. You pick up the mouth of the hose and you guide the water to the veranda, soaking the wooden panels, purifying the decks of any signs of sin. It is a veranda for angels now, and saints, too. You then take the stream of water to the middle of the yard where the tarp was, where you spilt a couple of bottles of red wine in a drunken frenzy. You let the water run until it floods the grass, turning the dirt into mud so that you couldn't tell it apart from the wine. You let this strange concoction drown the poor blades of grass and then disappear to the outskirts of the yard, just like Alejandro disappeared seven months ago.

You remember—

The curtains were still closed and the blankets were skewed, the top left corner of the comforter draped onto the floor. The bedroom was dim, but still bright enough for you to see the curves of Alejandro's face and the shape of the lavender comforter over his body. You considered grabbing a book from the pile on the floor by the door, and you could read while you waited for him to wake up. Instead, you stayed under the covers and watched his chest carefully rise and fall with his breaths, drunk with sleep. You're not sure how long you stayed there, watching him as if he were a sunrise, never taking your gaze off him in case you missed something completely glorious, like a fluttering eyelash or a sigh. When his eyes twitched and his face scrunched up into an artwork of broken sleep, you reached out and placed your hand atop his cheek, cupping his stubble.

"Good morning."

You watched his face smooth out into a warm smile. He craned his neck and kissed you, kissed you in your dim bedroom, injecting a hot sort of splash that trickled through your chest and into your stomach. Poisonous. He sat up, his back against the headboard, rubbed his eyes. You sat up, too, and opened the curtains, letting the mid-morning sunshine flood the room and mingle with the mess of the blankets on the bed. The sunlight even flirted with Alejandro's dark curls, arranged into the quintessence of bed-head. You felt content. If you'd died at that very moment, you wouldn't have minded, not really. It would have felt nice dying with the feeling of contentment nestled into the lines around your smile, as if that was the only feeling you'd feel ever again. Alejandro stretched an arm to the bedside table and picked up his phone. His thumb did some scrolling, did some tapping. The bedroom was glowing with sunlight, you remember it so clearly. That's one of your favorite things about that apartment, its accommodation of the sun, turning pebbles to gemstones, even if it didn't help anything grow. Staring intently at the screen of his phone, Alejandro frowned, then sat further upright, shimmying his bum. He started to tap with two thumbs now, *tap tap tap*. He looked at you, gaze lingering, then looked back down. The speed of his flickering gaze had whipped you, leaving you stinging.

"I have to go," he declared. His accent rolled off his tongue fantastically. "Something important has come up."

"Where are you going?" you asked.

A knock violently resounded from the front door. You

got up hastily, and Alejandro tried to stop you, clumsy and frantic. When you reached to open the door, you were faced with a towering man dressed in a three-piece suit, and his pistol, and his racing Spanish, and Alejandro slamming the door on him, and Alejandro kissing you on the forehead where a bullet was almost lodged just moments ago.

He pulled a T-shirt over his head, ran his fingers through his hair, and pulled on his jeans. He shoved his phone into his back pocket and made for the door.

"When will you be back?" you asked.

"I'll be back in no time, okay?"

"Okay. Bye."

"*Adiós.*"

And with that he left your apartment, shutting the door behind him.

You didn't see him again for six entire months, until he showed up at your doorstep, smelling of fabric softener and ruining your efforts to forget his name.

There were multiple occasions you had asked yourself whether you love Alejandro, or whether he was merely a man that made you feel like a woman. You had never managed to come up with a definitive answer; when you get close to answering, you force your thoughts to flit elsewhere. You remember once—someone, you can't exactly remember who—told you how easy it is to know whether you love someone or not. She said that when you see a pretty flower, like a geranium, perhaps, people are inclined to pluck it, so that they can bring it home or put it behind their ear to admire it, just because they like it so much. But if that person really loved the flower, they wouldn't pick it. Instead, they would let it grow, let it flourish, let it live. If someone truly loves a flower then they won't even touch it.

Tonight, as you hose your backyard, it is suddenly clear to you whether you love Alejandro or not.

You saw the flower and you picked it.

You turn off the tap and coil the hose back up. The sky, you notice, is beginning to lighten.

"I am sorry, Alejandro, I am so sorry," you say to the air in front of you, the air that had no choice but to witness this extraordinary night.

Pft. You are not sorry. You are extraordinary.

"Goodbye, Alejandro, *adiós.* It was hell knowing you."

You walk back inside the house, turn into your room, and crawl into bed.

Step 6

Ignore Time

(Time Is Merely A Social Construct, Anyway)

YOU SPEND THE NEXT three days in bed, engulfed in your duvet and swallowed by the dismal effect of the drawn blinds. You drift in and out of sleep, only ever venturing out of the covers to go to the bathroom. You keep a glass of water and a bowl of grapes on the vanity, rarely getting any use out of them. The thought of getting up and doing anything brings on migraines that densely soak your brain; throbbing, heavy and vile and inescapable throbbing. The only way to stop them is to fall back asleep.

The only thoughts you are able to consciously perceive is that Winnie is dead, *Winnie is dead*, and that you are a murderer, *yes, a murderer*. Sometimes your hand would find its way to your chest and you would hold the moonstone pendant between your thumb and index finger, thinking about how the moonstone must know your secret, too, just like the moon himself. Within those murky three days, it comforts you to know that you had a friend like the moonstone hanging from your neck that you could confide in whenever you wanted. Thinking about your confessions, though, also lured migraines, thick ones. At some point on the second day, you got up to apply lipstick, the wine-colored one from New York, and then you went straight back to bed. You'd like to think that looking a little bit different makes you different from the person you actually are. It's a stupid thought, really, but it's better than lying there looking completely like yourself. You'd like to think you have a bit of integrity.

At some point, though you're not entirely sure when, you remembered the stripped fingers that are sitting patiently in your freezer. You hurriedly flung the covers off your body and rushed to the bathroom, where you vomited into the toilet and then stayed on your knees staring into the toilet bowl a while longer, contemplating kneeling there for the rest of your life, your shins pressed hard against the cool tiles on the floor. When you finally went back to bed, you thought about how you may never find a warehouse sale ever again, not without Winnie. You thought about her vivid stories of Cravat and her intoxicating smile and her marble benchtops. She was a marvelous friend, was Winnie. You're sure that if you looked up the phrase 'best friend' in the dictionary, her name would be right there, defining the two words most appropriately. Such a splendid friend deserves to be reciprocated, and you'd like to think you were a good friend, you really do. But you used her special lemon verbena body wash and then disappeared. Quite frankly, you're no better than Alejandro, no matter how sickening that thought may be. You broke into her house, ate her lasagna, slept beneath her sheets, and abandoned her. Just like Alejandro broke into your head. Like he drank your tea. Like he slept in your bed.

Like he abandoned you.

Like your mother abandoned you.

Your brain is full of heavy, loud pulses that vibrate at your temples and shoot down your neck.

Stop thinking now, just stop.

Please go back to sleep.

       ❀   ❀   ❀

Your thoughts are scattered.

You can't quite

Seem to

Get a grasp on them.

And to reach out to them,

Oh, to reach out,

It hurts your head.

The throb of your pulse pelting beneath your jawline yells at you.

Give
Yourself
Attention
It yearns
With each harrowing throb
Do not disconnect.
Focus.

Lying in your bed, the smell of your own sweat clinging to the duvet, you feel overwhelmingly sad. As soon as you manage to get a slight grasp on your wandering thoughts, a dark cloud hovers over them, and your sadness amplifies. You must stop being dramatic, and start thinking about things logically. Getting rid of Alejandro benefits you. God knows what sort of business that man involved himself with, and if the police had found any slip ups, they would've connected you to him, they would've tracked you down, they would have shoved you into a sticky mess. Heck! If the police find out it was him who murdered Winnie, they'd track him down as quick as a hiccup, and their findings would lead them right to you. You see? Your decision was a very strategic, very necessary one, and allows you to keep your existence neatly buried. Just like Winnie might be buried right now. Oh, Winnie.

It is Sad, your predicament; it is Sad.

But at least it's lonely.

You should attempt to crawl out of the scattered and ruined debris of your feelings now. Take a shower and rinse the dust off.

Standing in the shower, letting the hot water drizzle down the slope of your back, you have an epiphany: Just like the sun, you were the day's antagonist. Just like the sun, you've become the day's protagonist. Just like the sun, no one noticed.

You feel overwhelming satisfied.

Accomplished, even.

You, my darling, are just like the sun.

You deserve a pat on the back. Maybe even a chocolate-coated strawberry, dark chocolate. Mmm, yes.

Out of the shower, your hair wrapped in a towel, you go to the kitchen and put a bowl of dark chocolate in the microwave. You take a punnet of strawberries out of the fridge and line a large plate with non-stick paper. The microwave beeps and you take the bowl out, stir the chocolate a couple of times. You coat the strawberries in chocolate and sit them on the plate, the chocolate shining like a manicure. Pop them into the fridge.

You're not sure what to do now. In the kitchen you just stand, thinking about nothing, thinking about everything. When do you think the strawberries will be ready? When you eat them, you should eat them with lips dressed in lipstick, it'll be more of a celebration. You wonder how Naomi's doing in New York. How long has she been there now? You don't know, you're not really keeping track. You go to your bedroom and find the wine-colored lipstick, and position yourself in front of a mirror. As you go to apply the makeup, you stop, the lipstick hovering just by your lips. You are staring into your very own eyes, the eyes of a stranger, really, the eyes of someone you have never made the effort to befriend. A thought occurs to you, an intellectual one, it seems, with no real reason or origin. Maybe it excuses the fact that you have never made the effort to befriend yourself. You have decided, quite suddenly, that a mask will not fix anything. It won't. Covering a flower in creams will turn the petals brown. Let your face find the sun. You replace the cap of the lipstick and put it down. How can you possibly be friends with yourself if you're only proud of yourself when you change the way you look? I think your body deserves an apology. Go on, take a long hard stare at yourself in the mirror.

Look at you, look how pretty you are.

You are the Sun.

I will not pluck you out of the ground, I will let you flourish. I love you.

And I am your friend.

You throw the lipstick in the bin.

Liberation, at last.

    ❧   ❧   ❧

In half an hour, you are out of the house and on your way to the shops, avoiding the cracks in the footpath. It is the first time you have ventured out of the house for a good couple of days, you're not sure how many exactly. You're a bit nervous to be out here. The thought of fraternizing with The Public compresses your chest and makes your eyes twitch.

Now that you love yourself, you are an alien.

You're not allowed to love yourself, you know that. You know from your own experience—you've always felt uncomfortable around people who are confident in themselves, because you know that nothing you do, and nothing you say, will ever really affect them. You become redundant. It has always been deemed as selfish to be confident in yourself, but it is not selfish, you realize, it is self-indulgent. It is appreciating that you are a delicacy. It is not having to rely on anyone else to tell you that you taste good. Delicately, you keep walking along the sidewalk, careful not to scuff your glaze. You chuckle softly, just to yourself. Oh, how you are scared.

A person walks by and you keep your gaze glued to the footpath. You should've held onto that stolen bike tighter, then you could ride it now and eye contact with passersby would be unnecessary. Still, you pretend eye contact isn't in your dictionary, and you pass thirteen people without daring to look up.

To your horror, one of them even bid you a good afternoon.

You nodded your head in return, just once. It was jerky and it strained your neck.

❀ ❀ ❀

In the heart of Waikiki, you pass a small nail salon, and you consider it. You didn't need lipstick this morning, but you wouldn't mind treating yourself to a mani-pedi. Maybe to love yourself isn't to reject the superficial additions. Maybe you're not trying to cover your flaws but enhance your beauty. Maybe you just want to give yourself a silly gift, just for fun. Maybe you don't have to be so decisive and be a little sympathetic towards your hypocrisy, like a kind person would. You can be kind. So, you step into the salon and treat yourself. You are the giver and receiver of gifts, the rising and setting of the sun. Now your nails are light pink, a bit like the color of the cotton-candy hair you once sported. You're a sucker for pink. Back on the street, you do some window shopping, aimlessly wandering and throwing glances of longing and admiration at items of clothing you are sure would look grand in your closet. When you pass Urban Outfitters, you stop to look at a leopard print slip dress with a cowl neck, the mannequin wearing it rather well. When you turn to continue walking, your shoulder pushes hard into someone else's and a rushed apology fumbles out of your mouth.

"Oh, my goodness," the woman says.

Uh-oh.

She reaches out and grabs your upper arm, clutches onto it and stands in front of your squarely.

"I'm sorry," you mumble again, "I wasn't looking where I was going and…"

"You're Denise's daughter, aren't you?" The question

slaps you, and you take a step back to absorb the impact. The woman is grinning now, a big toothy grin.

How dare she bring up your mother's name so unexpectedly.

"You don't remember me, do you?" She searches your eyes with her own. She's invading your privacy, and you want her to stop.

"I'm sorry," you repeat, sounding dumb, "I, uh…"

"It's me, Lani! I was Denise's best friend! When you were little I used to look after you and your sister all the time. Oh, you girls were so precious! I see Naomi every now and again but I haven't seen you in years! The last time I saw you must've been… well it must've been at Denise's funeral." Finally, the woman falls silent. She drops her hand from your arm. She drops her intense eye contact, too. Now you're both staring at the ground, letting shoppers push past you.

"Oh, I'm sorry, dear. I still miss her, too. She loved you so much, you know. When she talked about you and Naomi, her eyes twinkled. Oh, they twinkled so bright."

You look up at her and smile tightly. You want so badly for her to go away, for her to shut up. "Your hair," she says, speaking loud now, shoving jovial connotations into her words, "it's so modern and lovely. The black suits you."

"Thanks."

"We should get together for a coffee later; I want to hear all about what you've been up to for the past, well, it's been three years, hasn't it! It feels like a whole lifetime."

"I really must get going," you tell her, watching the smile slowly melt off her face and drip onto the footpath. "I'm sorry. Maybe, um, maybe another time."

"Yes, okay." You step around her and the puddle of her melted smile, and you walk away, leaving her behind like everything else from your past.

You keep on walking until you come across the shop of a hairdresser. Inside, you ask a man with long silky hair if there's someone available for you now, and after hesitating he sighs and tells you that, yes, there is, but it's much more practical if you make an appointment in the future. He ushers you to a seat and offers you a drink.

"I would love a lime and ginger tea, thank you."

He organizes his equipment while his assistant, a trainee, it looks like, boils the water.

"So," the man huffs, "What do you want done?"

"I'd like it dyed, please," you say. "Platinum blonde."

The hairdresser props his hands on his hips and sighs, heavily this time, his eyes rolling back into his head.

"Sweetie, if you're having an existential crisis, please spend your money on some proper counseling rather than a hairdo. It won't fix anything, trust me."

"But I'm not having a crisis."

"I know it's hard to accept, I see it all the time, really I do. But if you're going to manage it by dying your hair a tacky color, then at least save money and just do it yourself with the cheap stuff from Walmart."

"I told you," you veer, "I'm not having a crisis. Can you please just do your job?"

The man narrows his eyes and folds his arms close to his chest.

"Whatever. Fine. But don't come complaining to me when you're one hundred and ten dollars poorer and still stuck in a crisis."

Despite his refusals, the hairdresser does a good job on your hair, and you leave the salon with soft waves of platinum blonde falling gently around your shoulders. You are pleased. A bit relieved, too. You don't want to have any close encounters with your past like the one with Lani ever again, no siree Bob, not today, and not ever.

Back among The Public on the busy streets of Waikiki, you find that you are hungry, starving, even. Is it lunchtime yet? Or afternoon tea? You stop walking completely. What day is it? It's late January, you know that, but you can't recall what day it is. Let alone the time. This is supposed to stress you out, isn't it?

Isn't it?

But you don't feel stressed, you feel comforted.

How strange.

You feel comforted because… because… now you are living in reality.

Yes.

The thing is, the world has created structure by building clocks and calendars, and naming certain periods of time, like Monday and Saturday. This structure was created to bring comfort and rationality to human beings, but all it has done is thrust them into a false sense of living, into a constructed schedule that is perceived as Life. But it is not Life. It is deceit. Clocks and calendars and Tuesdays, they're all illusions. They're what have convinced you that you have a past. But what if the past hasn't even passed? When people want to eat, they starve not for the food itself, but for the time in which eating food is appropriate. Humans are fooled into thinking that the section of life labeled as the 25th of December is specifically designed for giving and receiving, fooled into thinking that eating when they see the numbers 12:30 is logical. But that's not logic, that's just ignorance. Logic is eating when your stomach growls softly, and your mouth slightly pools with saliva. Logic is having the capacity to give and receive whenever and wherever you want. In fact, it's so much more than logic; it's the capacity to be a human.

It's humanity.

Embedding time into society has programmed humans to function in sync. A bit like robots. And maybe you were a robot, too.

But now, you are human.

Your stomach hurts a bit, so you buy food, and you eat it.

Society can kiss your ass.

❧   ❧   ❧

The strawberries you put in the fridge earlier are set now. You take the plate out and place it on the benchtop, and you bring a chocolate-coated berry to your lips. Chewing it in your mouth, it tastes like hearts. You eat all of them, each of them exuberantly kissing the inside of your cheek. You are left with a small pile of wilted green leaves. You throw them out, useless, like your potential.

You take a seat on a lounge in the living room. You are very tired. You can feel the bags beneath your eyes sag; they weigh a lot, you can feel it now. In your silence, you notice a clicking sound, *click, click, click*. The clock on the wall. You heave yourself back up off the couch and wander to the wall, where you stand on your tippy-toes and hoist the clock off its hook. You take it to the kitchen, grab a pestle. With the pestle you smash the clock, you smash it as if it were society itself. As the glass shatters and the hands warp, the house begins to bathe in the calm of reality. You sit back down on the couch. Your silence is not interrupted.

Until.

The empty spot on the couch next to you indents, the leather creaking. You're not alone, you can sense it in the way your neck feels hot and your tongue yearns to say hello. A strong perfume hazes your thoughts, a perfume you're sure you've smelt before, a perfume that reminds you of...

Coupons.

And a smile, full of whiskey.

Yes, yes.

Winnie.

Suddenly you can hear the piano from the day you fled New York. You can hear it so loudly; the notes are vibrating against your skull.

You can hear the thud of books falling to the ground, one after another, echoing throughout the house.

You can hear the clink of the tiles on the rooftop, shrill and destructive.

And you can hear Winnie's voice. You can hear her say, *you're toast, you know.*

"Well, yeah," you whisper, "people who disappear aren't bread."

The indent on the couch slides closer to you.

"Were you in pain?" you ask to the air above the couch, the air drenched in perfume. "Were you in pain when Alejandro..." you can't finish your sentence. You can already feel her answer, it's compressing your lungs.

Yes.

"Sorry."

A question pours out of her, so tremendous that the silence it floats in shatters your eardrums, such thick and unforgiving silence.

Why didn't you tell me you wanted to leave?

Tears flood your eyes, hot ones that sting. If you answer her question, all it'll do is break both of your hearts.

"I'm so sorry," you say aloud, hardly audible. And then, just in your head, you think, *I didn't want to pluck you from your roots.*

The indent on the couch is gone now.

She is in heaven, you hope, her petals blooming.

        ❧ ❀ ❧

You're sick of this house. Sick of taking refuge in your bedroom. Every time you look at your lacy white duvet and the rickety vanity, you tremble, afraid that somehow you haven't changed, and that you never will. The air in this house, laden with the coconut scent of Naomi's moisturizer, is beginning to take its toll. It is suffocation. You are suffocating. In this house, the abused and the abuser have no differences—both live beneath your skin and grind against your teeth. One and the same.

If you stay here any longer, staring at the walls your mother once hung photo frames on, you will disintegrate.

There will be no one here to sweep the tiny pieces up.

They will stay ashen on the floorboards, dusty with guilt and fear.

You must escape before you disintegrate.

You have one very small problem, though, that could potentially prevent you from escaping. The thing is, you are poor. The last dregs of money have been scraped from your account, and the wad of cash Naomi strained to donate to you before she left has all been spent. You try to think if there's a spot in the house Naomi would stash some emergency money, but in the back of your mind you know that she's too organized to do such a thing. But wait—yes!—your mother wasn't so organized. No, your mother was nervous.

When you were about ten, she called you to her bedroom one day. When you got to the room she was sitting at the foot of her bed, looking so proud of you, so proud of her own creation.

"I want to show you something," she said. "I think you're old enough and responsible enough to see this, and that's why I waited until now. Don't mess it up, okay?"

The kindness in her eyes didn't match the stern flick of her words, but you nodded your head and felt your heart swell a bit with happiness, with responsibility. She led you over to a painting on the wall, a still life of a vase of wilting geraniums, and asked you to take it down. You looked at her, confused, but she just smiled. You did as you were told, uncovering the door of a safe. She pointed to the keypad and made sure you were paying attention.

"I'm going to tell you the password now, okay? So far, there are only two people in the whole wide world that know the password. You're going to be the third."

"Okay."

"You have to promise me that it stays at three, okay? You must promise me that you won't repeat the password to anyone, because it's a secret. You can keep a secret, can't you?"

"I promise, Mummy. I won't tell anyone, you can count on me."

She pressed the little square with the number three printed on it four times. "Did you see that?"

"Yes, Mummy. Three three three three."

"Good girl. Oh, I'm so proud of you." She smoothed your hair and planted a kiss atop your head. Her pride melted into you, it's warmth ran down your spine. She pressed the button labeled 'open,' and there was a click followed by the door swinging wide. You stood on your tippy-toes and peered inside. Straight away you noticed a thin pile of photographs, the top one depicting your mother and a man you vaguely recognized as your father. Before you could look at them properly, your mum's hand swooped in and snatched the pile quickly, stuffing it into her bra. "They're not supposed to be there," she mumbled. There was one more thing left in the safe, and she reached in and pulled it out, holding it in front of you as if it were the holy grail. Though it wasn't the holy grail, it was as close as you would get— she held a thick wad of cash, folded in half and held together by a rubber band. It was the size of a tennis ball. You stared at it, transfixed.

"How much is it?" you asked.

"That isn't important. What's important is that if you ever need help, if you're ever desperate and I'm not here, I want you to quietly come here and take it, okay?"

"Okay, Mummy."

"Don't tell anybody about it."

"I won't."

"Just use it to save yourself."

"Yes, Mummy."

You are in her bedroom now, taking down the painting. Sure, there's the possibility that Naomi might've taken the sacred ball of cash for herself, but she's too sentimental to do such a thing. You push the number three four times in a row and then push 'open'. The door swings open, and it's almost as if you are ten years old all over again, for when you peer inside, you are presented with a thin collection of photographs and the money. You pull out the photographs. The first photo is of a man and a woman, their arms wrapped around each other's shoulders and their heads leaning towards each other. Your mother's smile is courageous and authentic, woven into her eyes and plumping her cheeks. She looks young, seventeen maybe. The guy next to her doesn't look any older. His face is decorated with a sprinkling of freckles and a delighted smirk, handsome. You look so much like him it itches your eyes to look at the photo for much longer. You quickly flick through the rest of the photos, all of them taken at the same scene, both sitting on the edge of a park fountain, clear sky and curly cherubs. Looking at your parents, their bodies clutching onto each other, you wonder if they really loved one another.

You've only ever seen your father once. You were seven or eight, when he unexpectedly knocked on the door one night. Your mother answered and when she opened it you got a quick glimpse of him. The sight of him made you feel giddy, as if he were a forbidden room in the house. He began feasting on your mother, desperate and hungry. Your view of him was obscured then, but you got to hear his voice whisper a couple of times, you lucky thing, you got to hear his voice. After he finished his meal, his hair tousled and his lips shiny with your mother's lip gloss, he left, and your mother closed the door. When she turned, and saw you watching, she started to cry. You hated it when she cried.

"Daddy can't stay," she had said. "He says he's sorry."

That was the first and last time you ever saw him, and she never spoke of him again, not once.

You stuff the photos back in the safe and take out the money. You close the door and replace the painting.

"The thing is," you say, to the air that once touched your mother's skin, "I'm desperate and you're not here. So, I'm just going to use it to save myself."

You pack your few clothes in a duffel bag as well as your things from New York, and you leave the house, the house that has conjured so many memories in the past couple of weeks that it has made your knees weak. On the street, you hail a cab. Your mother would be so proud of you, doing something she never could. Saving yourself.

※   ※   ※

After some driving, you end up in the North Shore of Oahu, in Haleiwa. On the car trip, you counted the amount of money your mother had stashed—ten thousand dollars. You pay the driver and buy yourself a shave ice, lips numb against the cold. You used to come up here with your mum and sister for day trips and weekend getaways. In winter, you'd perch yourselves on the road above Waimea Bay and watch the thirty-foot waves lick the surfers up and eat them whole, and in summer you'd lay on the beach, either at Pipeline or Sunset, eating food from cardboard boxes and decorating yourselves with tan lines. This part of the island oozes with isolation, and it kisses your bear arms and soothes your nerves. Chickens cluck down the uneven roads and the locals pad to and fro to the beach, bare feet and beaten surfboards. Sun showers are regular blessings. This is the place to be.

You head over to the real estate agency, the only real estate agency on this side of the island, and you ask about available holiday houses, preferably right on the beach. The man at the desk slowly moves his fingers across the keyboard, jabbing at the keys, and then turns the ancient computer screen around to face you. He takes you through the options, his own attention meandering every now and again.

When he finishes, he says, "As you can see there are plenty of bangers, but really it's up to you."

You end up picking a villa right on Sunset Beach, and instead of giving you the keys, the man instructs you to drive on up and knock on the door, where the villa's owner will greet you and make sure you settle in. You thank him for his help and scurry onto the street.

You walk along the road with your thumb sticking out, and soon enough you're hitching a ride from a man named Bruce in his pick-up truck. As soon as you plop into the passenger seat, your bags piled on your lap, Bruce starts talking. He talks non-stop. He talks about his wife, Lucy, who is allergic to cats and makes a killer sweet potato pie. He talks about his surfboard, which he hand-carved all by himself and has prided himself in never dinging it, not once. He even talks about the awful haircut he got when he was sixteen, you think he said it was a bowl-cut, and how he wishes he could pretend it never happened but it's in all his homecoming photos and he doesn't want to forget about homecoming. He manages to fit all this information into a matter of moments, each and every second seeming longer and longer. Though as much as it pains your ears to listen to such fickle ramblings, you enjoy the fact that you were expected to stay silent the whole trip, nodding your head respectfully a couple of times and chucking in a couple of *wows* and *ohs*.

When Waimea Bay comes into sight, you ask Bruce to drop you off in the beach's carpark, and you thank him for the ride. In the carpark, you buy a choc-top from an ice cream truck. When you bite into it, the chocolate shell fractures and you lick up the shards before they fall. You take a seat on the sand, your attention launching to the winter swell. Mountains of water erupt before you, curling into thick frothy lips and devouring anything and everything in their path. They are waves not measured in feet or meters but in increments of fear. It's a marvelous show Mother Nature has put on for you, simply breath-taking. It's hard to take your eyes off the ocean; watching the movement of the mountains is delicious and addictive. Mists of sea spray splash your face and leave a fine layer of salt on your skin, like armor, like a gift. Sitting here, witnessing such artistry, it is humbling. It makes you feel so damn tiny, so insignificant. You are but a brief flicker of movement in this great big world that spins and spins without ever getting dizzy. You are unnecessary, yet you are here, living and breathing and deciding each morning what to eat for breakfast. Right now, staring at Mother Nature's masterpiece, you are certain that the ocean was put upon earth with purpose. You are also certain, well... almost certain, that you might have some purpose, too. Because why else would you be here, taking up oxygen and seating space on the sand? Anybody else could've done this in your place. They could've marveled at the waves and caught shards of chocolate with their tongue. You, you existential bastard, are incredibly significant within this vast insignificance.

Your significance is entirely dedicated to yourself.

You are here for you,

Not them.

There is a warm twinkling in your stomach, a smile latches onto your lips, too. Look at the waves, look at the mighty waves.

And look at you.

I am so proud of you.

Step 7

Spread Falsities and Fabrications

THE AFTERNOON'S AIR IS warm and patting you softly as you wait on the doorstep of your holiday villa on the shore of Sunset Beach. You've rang the doorbell twice now, and even knocked once. You are just about to ring the bell a third time when the door clicks open and reveals an old lady, her stature tiny and frail, wrapped in an apron like a birthday present. She peers up at you through her glasses, the canals of her wrinkles thick with makeup. Her lipstick is bleeding into the puckered crevices around her mouth. The lines that trace her face, they are like a map of everywhere she's been. It is a beautiful, intricate map, one which tells stories and holds memories. It is a valuable face, gorgeously valuable.

One day you hope your face is valuable, you hope it whispers to anyone that dares to look at it, *look where I have been. Look where I have risen from.*

Suddenly, words rush from her mouth. They are cursive and smooth and indecipherable, and they leave you staring at the way her lips dance with her tongue to create such symphony.

"*Ho appena ricevuto la chiamata dall'agenzia immobiliare, non ho avuto molto tempo per prepararmi, nessun tempo, ma tutto sarà pronto a breve, non ti preoccupare, non ti preoccupare.*" Her words are bathing you, baptizing you, a hasty blessing that isn't important enough to linger over but still worthy of listening to.

Finally, the woman stops to take a breath and pushes her thick-rimmed glasses up the bridge of her nose. "*Parli Italiano?*" she croaks.

"Um… I'm, uh… my name is Cille," you tell her. You don't sound very sure of yourself. You must sound sure of yourself, otherwise she'll know. You know she'll know, old ladies like this one have a sixth sense. She squints her eyes as she wonders what you just told her, her mouth slightly hanging open.

"*Vieni dentro, per favore, vieni dentro.*"

The woman turns around and shuffles into the house. You wipe your feet on the doormat and follow her in before losing sight of her around a corner. The villa is spacious and airy, bamboo ceiling fans hanging high above your head and the rooms furnished with beech-wood and palm fronds. The windows are dressed in white Venetian blinds, window sills spotted with tiny potted plants and odd seashells.

Suddenly, the old lady is right in front of you again, pushing a cheek of a mango into your hands, its flesh scored. She licks the pulpy juice off her bony fingers and waits patiently for you to eat. You invert the skin and the mango pops up. You bite off a square, the flesh kissing your chin.

"I manghi sono ormai molto maturi, così dolci e succosi."

As you eat, you stare at a painting on the wall in front of you, a scene of a narrow stone-flagged street embraced by squashed rectangular buildings, each of them their own color. The lady follows your gaze to the quaint ambient painting and she smiles, showing a mouth full of crooked teeth.

"Questa è Venezia, da dove vengo. Questa è casa mia."

Despite your complete lack of understanding, you nod, you smile, you finish the mango. The old lady totters away into the kitchen. You are left standing halfway between the living room and the corridor, waiting.

❧   ❧   ❧

Sitting at the dining table, your hand fiddling nervously with a serviette, you watch as the old lady fills the table with food. She places down a tray of lasagna, a bowl of Arancini, a plate of risotto, a basket of bread and a bottle of red wine. She wipes her hands down her apron and sits down. She is sitting at the head of the table, awkwardly far from you. You watch her, you can't take your eyes off her, she is fascinating. She is like a tourist attraction. She presses her hands together and closes her eyes. She mumbles beneath her breath, rapid curls of Italian rolling off her tongue and forming a prayer. You press your hands together, too, as you watch on. Then she opens her eyes again and she's back on her feet and leaning across the table to reach the food, piling her plate high. She looks up at you, stares for a moment, then gestures at the food, gestures at your plate. You repeat what she did until your plate is full, and when you finish she opens the wine bottle and fills both your glasses.

"*Buon appetito*," she smiles to you.

The old lady picks up her fork and stabs it into an Arancini ball, bringing it to her mouth and nibbling at it with her puckered lips.

Between mouthfuls, the old lady says, "*Il mio nome è Donna-Maria.*" She must be telling you her name, you're sure of it.

"My name is Cille," you tell her again.

Donna-Maria looks at you, expressionless, then looks back down at her food. The clatter of forks against plates finds a home within the silence. You swallow a mouthful of risotto and look back up at Donna-Maria. Her glasses are sliding down the bridge of her nose. You open your mouth to tell her, then stop. She wouldn't understand you; it's pointless. Instead, you start telling her something else.

"I'm on vacation here in Hawaii, you see, I'm from Australia, born and raised, and my parents are both French, and I'm an only child, and I live with my dad, you know, every day he drives me to university, and he picks me up, too, except for now, of course. It's the summer holidays in Australia, I love my dad, you know, he's the best dad out there, and you know what else? He makes the best fish tacos you've ever tasted, you should try them one day, anyway, I'm studying philosophy at university, a Bachelor of Arts with a Major in Philosophy, I love it, you know, I…"

Take a breath.

What do you think you're doing?

Stop yourself, control yourself.

"I have a boyfriend, back at home, his name's Richmond and he has these great big hands that play the piano terrifically, and I cook for him! I'm a great cook, I can even tell apart coriander from parsley, that's how good I am, and while I cook Richmond plays with the dogs, yes, we have seven Chihuahuas, and each of them have a sweater a different color of the rainbow, isn't that cute? And this is my natural hair color, one hundred percent natural, people always pass me and tell me how interesting my hair is, isn't it interesting? I have a job, too, I make lots and lots of money, you wouldn't believe it for a girl my age, as a matter of fact just the other week I bought an apartment in New York City—I bought it!—I own a cat, too, a black one like a witch's kitty and he doesn't have opposable thumbs, and not too long ago, I was in a car with two of my friends, Alex and Welma, we were driving along, and we crashed, a big, *big* crash, and both of them died, Alex and Welma died and…"

Your cheeks are wet.

Why are your cheeks wet?

You're crying… why are you making yourself cry!

Shut up.

Shut up.

"I am still alive." Your voice is tiny now, slipping into shadows cast by the crockery on the table. "Welma died first, and then Alex. I stayed alive. They didn't have to die—they didn't even have to get in the car. But they did. For me. They got in the car for me. I didn't even tell them to get in the car, you know, I didn't actually want them in the car in the first place. The headlights shattered though, and the bonnet crumpled like a piece of scrap paper. There was a lot of blood, too. So much blood. It has stained my eyelids, the insides of them. When I close my eyes, all I see is red. Red red red. Not the red of a rose, but the red of raw meat. Fleshy and torn and angry. They're dead now, forever. Do you think it's my fault?"

Donna-Maria is looking down at her food, pushing grains of rice round and round her plate. Your nose is snotty and wet, and your vision is cloudy with tears and distress. Donna-Maria looks up from her food and your hopes flinch. You watch as she reaches her crooked hand out to her wineglass and takes a long, wobbly sip. She doesn't seem to have registered your question. In fact, it's as if you never even opened your mouth.

Uncontrollably, you start to wail. Big, sopping gulps that shake your rib cage and twist your face. Your sobs echo violently against your eardrums, hands clenched into futile fists, barren fists. Donna Maria looks up. Looks at you. Your breath wavers.

"Non c'è bisogno di piangere, bambina. Avere un po 'di fede. Non so cosa diavolo hai appena detto, ma sono sicuro che la fede lo risolverà."

You blink a couple of times, pushing tears down your cheeks, watching Donna-Maria wipe the corners of her mouth with a serviette. You have no idea what she just said, and you hate yourself for it. That mess that just poured out of your mouth, that sickening, decadent mess, is sitting heavily between you two, both of you slowly soaking it in.

"I'm sorry," you murmur, mostly to yourself, "I... I didn't mean to talk so much. Sorry."

Donna-Maria looks to you and nods, feigning understanding.

❧　❧　❧

You're not tired enough to go to bed, and you don't want to hang around Donna-Maria, so you open up the big glass double doors at the back of the house and you wander into the backyard, the dusky night air balmy against your shoulders.

The yard is scattered with mango trees, the trees wearing big orange lobes of mangoes like earrings, some bulbous and ripe and others only fetal. Leaning against the back of the house is a tall wooden ladder which has been completely consumed by a passionfruit vine, the twisting thing adorned with shiny purple fruit and dainty little flowers. In the far corner of the backyard grows a big frangipani tree, it's thick canopy choked with pink-tipped frangipanis. In a way, it reminds you of your mother's front yard.

You pluck a flower and tuck it behind your ear.

You think about what just happened at dinner, wincing at the recollection. In the end, people only know what they are told, and what they know becomes fact; they don't know any better. This mess that spilled from your mouth, it has been received as truth, mistakenly delivered as fact rather than delusional fantasy.

Oops.

You have to admit though, as much as the rush of words overwhelmed you, it charged you with a sort of adrenaline shock that buzzed you into a new type of comfort. It has put a new possibility within your reach, one that is always looming on the horizon even though its proper place should be far, far behind you. It is the possibility that out of this mess you might be able to pluck out one thing: your past. Your past, in all its nostalgic, agonizing glory, it's haunted melody and sour aftertaste, you could once and for all put it to bed. You hate tripping on it over and over, knowing that it's right there in front of you and yet you still trip nevertheless. You're tired of seeing its reflection in everything you look at. You want to be able to look around this garden and watch the flowers with your thoughts at ease, without your stomach turning to water. Most of all, you want to enjoy being yourself. There is simply no point in loving yourself if you are always so conscious of your flaws, so terrified that they'll leap out of and consume your whole being, until all that is left is your withered, grey soul. If you are to love yourself, you must do so entirely; you mustn't watch the deterioration of your mind—that is sadistic, that is unbearable. Please, instead of watching, help your mind. Whisper to her words of kindness. Tell her how important she is, how courageous. Tell her... tell her it's okay to let go. See how her hands are red raw from holding on so tight? See the blood blisters and the swollen calluses? Tell her it's okay to let go. Tell her to have faith in the matter within you that was created by the stars, and crafted so delicately and lovingly. Tell her, tell her right now, to grab a carving knife, and start shaping someone she is proud of, someone she is willing to love every single day. Don't worry, you will still be made of the same celestial matter, you will still fundamentally be exactly who you were made to be, but it'll be on your terms, to your measurements.

Imagine how proud the stars are, eh? Imagine how proud the stars would be knowing their atoms created someone like you.

This is the proper beginning of loving yourself.

This is the beginning of a Revolution.

※　※　※

You spend the next couple of weeks meandering from the holiday house to the beach and back, endlessly adjusting the strap of your swimsuit and picking sand from underneath your toenails. Every now and again Donna-Maria silently shuffles into the house to restock the pantry or fix up your unmade bed, her services being something you weren't aware were included in your payment. On the days it is too hot to make the short trip to the beach you lay in the shade of the mango trees, rubbing the salt out of your eyebrows from your swim the day before, and when your manicure begins to chip you pick at that, too. Your skin gets tanner and your swimsuit thinner, and your bleached hair gets dry and crispy. Most days you don't even bother opening your eyes all the way; your eyelids rest half closed, too lazy to battle the Hawaiian sun in its fight for heroism. When you're hungry you ignore the prepared meals Donna-Maria has stacked in the fridge, and you opt for roasted almonds or cinnamon Pop-Tarts, or when you feel extra motivated you cut open a passionfruit or mango from the garden. You don't talk to anyone, not even Donna-Maria, you just listen to the voices inside your head and the distant crash of waves on the shoreline. One time, when you were walking from the kitchen to the bedroom, you spotted a clock on the wall, and calmly you took it down and popped it in the bin. These weeks are very serene, very unremarkable. They leave you feeling sleepy and poetic, though the poetry seems to reach no further than your hushed thoughts and the sleep seems to flow like a river, luring you to your salty bed much too often. When you wake up it's always too hot, leaving you sticky and delirious.

One particular night, when the river of sleepiness momentarily lapses, you wander into the bathroom and find six sachets of face masks under the vanity, each of them claiming a different purpose. You try them all, and by the end your face is stinging and you still aren't tired. That's when you notice that your swimsuit, which you haven't changed out of once, is beginning to smell of old seaweed and sweat. You step out of it and flick it into the washing machine, not bothering to actually turn it on, and throw on a sundress. You find your wallet from the diner in New York and step out of the house into the mystique of the night, moonlight reflecting off your shiny, stinging face. You begin walking up the road, walking and walking and walking.

You don't know how long you walked for, nor do you really care, but by the time you stop you are slicked in sweat and standing in front of an immense resort, the exterior illuminated by spotlights nestled into the masterful landscaping. You walk into the lobby, very quiet, footsteps absent atop the carpet. Besides you, the lobby is empty. The lights are bright, especially against the ebony of the night sky just outside. If someone were to tell you right now that you were the only person that existed, you would believe them. As far as you're concerned, all that has purpose in existing in this very moment is the harshly lit lobby, the armchair you have just seated yourself in, and the body in which you reside. You cannot see anything else and you do not desire anything else, therefore the whole entire universe has been reduced to this luminescent lobby. See outside? There is nothing there, nothing beyond the lobby doors, but a black void. An endless abyss. You are no longer a speck. You have the whole world to yourself, just because it pleases you for it to be that way. You sink further down into the armchair, chin bowing into your chest at the base of your neck. You take a deep breath. A river of vigorous sleep once again rushes down your spine and between your joints, and promptly your entire world is reduced to the insides of your eyelids.

You wake up and your posture jolts upright, hands clutching onto the padded arms of the chair. The lobby is peppered with people, some at the reception desk and others loitering around the corridor entrances. Looking out the large lobby doors, you can see that the universe in which you exist spans for kilometers, sunny and green and caring. You rub your eyes and stand up, pondering what to do next. You are hungry, you're sure of that, so you should probably find some place to eat. You exit the front door of the lobby and walk around the side of the resort, craning your neck to look up at the flashing array of windows and balconies draped in beach towels across the resort's exterior. You turn left to the back of the resort, where there is a glittering swimming pool, framed with deck chairs and sun umbrellas. Little kids strapped in goggles pester their parents to join the fun, flicking splashes of water onto their legs. The children's pleas are only returned with bribes. *I will only come and play if you put on more sunscreen*, they say, *and I'm not getting my hair wet. I will only come and play if you do not get my hair wet.* You ought to pour a whole bucket of water over those parent's heads, and steal their sunscreen, too. Your mother never would have bribed you like that, never.

Keep looking for food.

You pass the pool and walk further along a little footpath lined with exotic, healthy plants, passing a few tourists wrapped in beach towels and strolling along in their flip-flops. The path fades and leaves you in front of—yes!—a restaurant!

You find the entrance and stride in. Almost instantly you are stopped by a waitress.

"*Aloha*! Welcome to The Conch! Do you have a reservation?"

"Uhh," you strain your neck to look at the diners. All of them are definitely older than forty, women wearing pearl necklaces and the men sporting gelled hair and pressed button-downs. Your heart sinks. You couldn't possibly go in there looking like this, and you didn't intend on spending thirty dollars on a snack.

"I think I got the wrong cafe. I was supposed to meet

a friend for lunch somewhere around this resort, but it's so big I can't seem to find it! What did you say this restaurant was called again?"

"Oh, don't worry," the waitress giggles kindly, "that happens all the time! Honestly, you'd be surprised how many people come in here lost. Did your friend say anything about The Conch?"

"No." You put on your thinking face, eyebrows furrowed. You are a Museum of Contemplation. Exquisite, darling. Good job. "He didn't say anything about a restaurant, I think. It must've been a cafe or a kiosk or something. That's what I dressed for, anyway!"

The waitress kindly laughs again, this time pressing her tanned hand against her chest. "You must've been talking about Sandy Toes! It's the kiosk by the bay on the other side of the resort, right on the sand. Don't worry, it's not too far from here. Just walk towards the pool…"

You follow the waitress's directions, and soon enough you're standing in front of Sandy Toes. The smell of hot chips makes your stomach growl impatiently. You order some food and sit yourself down. You look out onto the glinting water of the cove, eating and eavesdropping. One particular conversation clutches to your attention and you home in on it.

"It's all the way from the Cook Islands," a lady's voice boasts from behind you. Discreetly, you twist around. On the table behind you a woman with soft grey curls and red fingernails is leaning in close to three children sitting with her, her grandchildren, perhaps. All the kids are staring straight at her chest in awe, fixated. "The kind lady who sold it to me explained that it's supposed to protect the wearer from negative energy, and it carries healing powers. She explained that they're very rare, so rare that *wayyyy* back in the olden days, they were only worn by royals and nobles."

The three kids *ooo* and *ahhh*, and then one asks,

"Can we see it up close, grandma?"

"Oh, all right then, but you must be very gentle, because it's very precious to grandma."

"We will!" they all chorus.

The woman reached behind her neck, her hands diving beneath her curls, and produces a necklace. You strain your eyes to make out the pendant, it definitely looks unfamiliar, but you think it's a… yes it must be a… a black pearl! How sensational! The woman dangles it in front of the children, and they all take turns touching it. You want to touch it, too, you want to be sitting with the children, wishing and hoping and praying that the pearl's healing powers will seep into the pads of your fingers and into your bloodstream. You want to be healed; you want to be the healer. The woman is fastening the necklace back around her neck now, and like the kids, your gaze seems to be super-glued to it.

The hot chips are brought to your table and you eat them rapidly, lips salty and fingertips greasy.

"Let's go change into our bathing suits now, yeah?" the lady chirps to her grandchildren. "We can go for a snorkel!"

"Maybe we'll find a pearl!" cheers one of them.

The lady laughs and brushes the tip of her finger against his little button of a nose. "Maybe!"

Once the four of them are up and walking, you get up too, and you follow them. Keep a distance, though, don't be weird about it. You trail them back up the footpath and up the side of the resort, all the way back into the lobby. They're all holding hands, all clinging onto each other. It triggers a longing within you for something you never had, an unfulfillable desire. Stop looking at their hands and just follow them, goddammit. You're so damn sensitive, just stop. Please. Your sensitivity is obnoxious. Okay, focus now. The family head to the lifts, the kids battle to press the button, and then they wait. You wait, too, just a little way off. Should you get in the same lift as them? Would that be too obvious? It's not like its unusual to go in a lift with other people—everyone does that all the time. And you don't want to risk losing track of them, because how would you know what floor they'd get off if you didn't go with them? But you can't act lost, either. If you go in the lift with them, you have to look like you know where you're going. There's a *bing* and the doors of the lift open. Okay, don't mess this up. The family shuffle into the lift and you follow suit. The kids battle again to press the button. Once they step back you note that they pressed level three. You step forward to press a button, hesitate, then remark, "Oh, I'm on level three, too!"

"It's a great view from up there, don't you think!" The lady says.

"Yes, it's fantastic," you agree.

Everyone falls into silence, the kids squirming. *Bing.* You step back to let the family out first, the lady smiles at you warmly, and you follow behind, keeping your distance. They walk down the corridor, every now and again stopping to point at something outside the large windows. Finally, they stop at a door and pull out a key. They file into the room, you wait for the click of the door shutting. You stroll up to the door; it is room 137B. Remember that, okay? 137B.

You turn around and head back to the lifts. You press the button, wait, and *bing.* The lift opens and out walks a young teenage girl with straggly hair swept into a messy ponytail, dressed in a uniform that suggests she's a cleaner or room service of some sort, pushing a trolley full of cleaning supplies and linen. You sneak a glance at her nametag, and yes, on it is the logo of the resort.

Before you allow yourself to think much further, you blurt, "Um, hi, excuse me?"

She stops and smiles at you. "Yeah?"

"Hi. Today is my first day on the job, but I seem to have misplaced my uniform and I can't find it anywhere. Ugh, I'm so embarrassed. I haven't even finished a single shift and they're already gonna fire me!"

The girl laughs awkwardly. "No one's going to fire you; it happens plenty. Um… I have a spare uniform in my locker… I guess you can borrow it if you want?"

"Are you sure?"

"Uh, yeah, I only really have it there as a backup

anyway." A strand of hair falls in front of her face and she quickly tucks it back behind her ear, her gaze rushing around the corridor nervously.

"Thank you so much! I'll return it as soon as I get my own again, I promise. Do you, um, do you think you could remind me how to get to the lockers again? It's such a big resort and I don't wanna get lost..."

"It's not... that big."

"Oh, I know, but I just wanna be sure. Don't wanna risk another big mistake on my first day!" The girl gives you some quick, choppy directions, apologizing every time she accidentally tells you to go left instead of right.

"Thanks..." you sneak another look at her nametag, "...Becky. I'll see you around. Oh, I'm Cille, by the way."

You stick out your hand and she shakes it warily, her own hand damp and hot. "I better start cleaning..."

She gives you a smile half-heartedly and begins pushing her trolley up the corridor. Right, then. Good on you. You just got yourself a job.

❦ ❦ ❦

You found your way to the lockers easily enough, and now that you have the uniform on you feel like a qualified con artist.

Con artist.

Look at that—you're an artist.

An inventor of beauty.

A hustler.

The curation of your very own thoughts is an artwork in itself, the exploitation of your thoughts becoming the masterpiece.

The Masterpiece.

You are a Masterpiece.

It is all so colorful, too, so expertly put together.

Look at the vermilion of your cunning, the azure of your deceit. Look at how the fuchsia of your guile looks so perfect against the marigold of your liberation.

Your brain belongs in an art gallery.

It should be framed, framed in heavy, curly brass, it's colorful fluid dripping, oozing from the crevices. People would want to reach out and touch it. People would want to have the colorful fluids run down their fingers and past their wrists. They'll want it to drip right down to their elbow, thick and pungent and striking. Their tongues would twist out of their mouths and lick your brain fluid off their arms, they would stick their fingers into their mouths and scrape the juices off with their teeth, excesses of it dribbling down their chins. Just imagine the streams of vermilion and azure and fuchsia and marigold swirling into people's saliva and getting caught underneath their fingernails.

She is an artist, they would chant. *She is a masterpiece. She is both the creator and the creation.*

You are both the creator and the creation.

You take a supply trolley and wheel it up to the third floor. You walk up the corridor until you get to room 137B, retrieving the key card from a pocket on the trolley.

You knock on the door and holler, "Housekeeping!" No one answers.

They must already be back down at the bay. Good.

You knock again, just to be sure. "Housekeeping!" No answer. So, you let yourself in.

The doorway opens into a spacious room, two king beds dressed in coral-blue comforters pressed against the right wall and a large television mounted on the left. Immediately to your right is the bathroom, speckled in tiny aquamarine tiles and perfectly polished. Beyond the beds and T.V. are two armchairs, a coffee table, a wardrobe, and beyond that are two glass sliding doors that give way to a balcony and a view of the left side of the resort; the shoreline of the island. You shut the door behind you, lock it, and wait a few moments to take everything in. You take in the bath towels sprawled across the armchairs and the dirty panties piled on the floor by the bed. You take in the array of bottles and tubes on the vanity in the bathroom, the display of pamphlets splayed across the coffee table. And you take in the necklace bearing a black pearl, haphazardly scrunched atop a bedside table. You hurry across the room, not caring for disturbing the pile of undies on your way. And then there it is, barely centimeters from your fingertips. *I can heal you*, it whispers. *I will heal you. I will heal you so thoroughly that the biggest power you shall possess is the power to heal others. Healers are the healed*, it says.

You pick it up, the chain unraveling delicately,

the pendant hanging. You undo the clasp and go to put it around your neck—but wait—there is already something around your neck. There is a moonstone. It probably knows all your secrets by now. It has probably been listening to you this whole time, ever since you plunged that wretched knife into Alejandro's sculpted chest. All your flaws are held within the milky complexion of this pendant. The moon listens to everyone's secrets, *everyone's*. There is no such thing as hiding from the moon, just as one cannot hide from God, and here you are wearing it around your neck, just as a Christian would wear a cross. You rip the necklace from your neck, run out onto the balcony, and throw it as far as you can. You are done being listened to. You are done being connected to your weaknesses, to your sins. You fasten the black pearl around your neck. I love you, therefore you will heal until you are like the warp of a scar, inimitable and incomparable.

You will heal.

You leave the room, taking a bottle of charcoal cleanser on your way out. Pushing the trolley in front of you, you head all the way back down to the locker room, where you grab your clothes and ditch the trolley. Into the lobby, out the front doors, onto the road. You walk all the way back to the villa, your skin itchy with sweat beneath the uniform. You walk with the piercing blue sky watching over you, with strong, healthy trees marching beside you like soldiers, with a couple of stray chickens clucking past you in a frenzy. You walk, you walk, you walk.

When you get back to the villa, you let yourself in and find Donna-Maria peeling mangoes at the kitchen counter. At your arrival, she looks up from the fleshy fruits, eyes you up and down, the pattern of lines in her face barely moving, as if she were a sculpture. She keeps on peeling the mangoes.

"I got a job," you say, not expecting a response, just saying it for the mere sake of it, like everything you do, really.

Donna-Maria shuffles over to the fridge and pulls out a crock-pot, places it atop the counter. When she takes off the lid the scent of its contents hits you hard and fast, a stupendous slap, and you almost stumble. It is chili con carne, just like what your mother used to make, just like Naomi tried to make. Donna-Maria begins to spoon the concoction into a bowl, pops it in the microwave, then pulls it back out after the beep. She waddles to you and gently takes you by the shoulders, guiding you to take a seat at the dining table. You don't say anything. All you can think about is the way your nose used to run while you ate it, and how your mum would laugh—she had such a full laugh— and she would take a serviette and wipe your dribbling nose. What if your nose runs now? What will you do then? What will you do when your mother's laugh is replaced by ringlets of Italian words? What will you do when you have to wipe your own nose? Donna-Maria places the bowl in front of you along with a fork and a glass of milk. It smells like you are fourteen years old.

You pick up the fork and dunk it into the bowl. You scoop up a mouthful, and you eat it.

You eat it.

And another mouthful.

And another.

You eat until there is nothing left in the bowl.

When your nose runs, you wipe it against the shoulder of your uniform.

Easy.

See how easy that was?

See how okay it is to let go?

It is okay to let go.

Step 8
_____

Fall into the Shadows, Like a Myth, Like a Secret

FOR THE NEXT FEW weeks, or maybe it is months, you go back and forth to the resort, wearing the uniform and pushing around a trolley full of cleaning supplies. In the rooms, rather than making beds and replacing towels, you steal drawstring bags filled with earrings and cameras filled with photos of smiling faces and lush scenes. You take watches and passports and leather purses and cash. Lots and lots of cash, some of it even foreign. You stuff your findings into laundry bags until they bulge, and you stuff the trolleys with filled laundry bags. At the end of each day you take everything back to the villa, sometimes hitching a ride and other times hopping in a cab on its way back to the airport. At the villa, you stash everything in your bedroom, cascading piles of purloined pieces fringe the outskirts of the room like a treasure trove. The nights Donna-Maria isn't home to cook dinner, you hitch a ride back up to the resort, dressed in stolen attire, and you dine at The Conch, your hair neatly styled and your cutlery skills impeccable. Nobody takes a second glance at you. You fit in like a mosaic tile. Some nights you wear diamond earrings with a matching diamond hair-clip, paired with a sleek black dress, and other nights you wear a ring bearing a prodigious, clean-cut ruby. You always, always wear the black pearl necklace.

The few times people attempt to strike a conversation with you, you pull out the photograph of seven Chihuahuas, and you tell them to look at your puppies that are waiting for you at home, look how sweet they are in their sweaters, and the people just coo and laugh and return to their meals. Every night you dine at the Conch, a family of four sits in the very middle of the restaurant. They attract stares like a magnet. The father, whose chest hair pokes out of his singlet, only ever opens his mouth to argue with his eldest son, whose attention is given solely to the iPad fixed between his thumbs. He looks about seventeen years old. The mother, her voice irritatingly nasal, comments on how tasty the food is, mostly to herself, mostly to penetrate the silence that they are drowning themselves in. The youngest son, maybe fourteen years old, does not wear a single expression on his face other than complete lethargy, his fuzzy face swollen with acne. Sometimes the argument between the father and his eldest son gets too loud, and the mother whimpers, and the father gets up and walks to the bathroom, his shorts caught in his inner thigh exposing white, pudgy masses of hairy flesh. It makes a couple of the diners gag every time. This family, this family that is watched as if they are a car crash, does not live. They exist, but they do not live. You can tell by the way the father uses his fingers to wipe spilt Fanta onto the floor. This family stopped living as soon as the man and the woman married each other in the name of convenience, you can just tell. And when they finish their meal and the diners eye them quietly as they leave the restaurant, the mother quickly gets out her phone and, while the rest of the family isn't looking, takes photos of the sky in a desperate attempt to know what it feels like to live again. She doesn't have time to look back at the photos though, so what is the point? Observing this lifeless family makes you realize: disappearance is all well and good as long as you continue to live. Existing is not enough. You are significant to yourself, remember? Plain existence is the same as death. You must continue to live.

❧   ❧   ❧

Tonight, you are eating dinner at the villa. Donna-Maria has prepared home-made fish fingers with some sort of Italian sauce, which is the most Western thing she's ever cooked. At the dinner table you both eat quietly, making sure every last morsel of food is scraped off the plate. When you finish, you say, "The fish fingers were delicious, thanks." You do not expect a reply, nor do you want one. You never expect one, never want one.

"Fingers."

You look at the old woman. Did she just say a word in English?

"Fingers." Sure, her voice is wobbly and creaks a bit, but it just spoke English. You're not quite sure what to do with this conversation.

"Yes," you tell her, "the fish fingers, they were great."

"Fingers," Donna-Maria squeaks, the consonants jarring tightly, "Fingers, fingers, fingers."

"Er, yeah, fingers. Fish fingers."

This conversation has gone too far for your liking; it's making you uncomfortable. A little hot, too. And Donna-Maria says contently, "fingers," and you say, "fish fingers," and then you say, "fingers."

Fingers.

Oh, God, fingers.

Goddamned fingers!

No.

Jesus Christ, fingers!

You moron.

You worthless moron.

Alejandro's fingers.

You left them in Naomi's freezer.

Goddammit.

You stand abruptly, knocking the chair over. You

stumble to your room, grab a wad of cash and your copy of the house keys and you stash them in your bra. Out the front door, onto the road, walking southbound. When you hear the rumble of a car engine you get ready to wave your arms about, and when you do the car pulls over and you slide into the backseat. You don't bother to greet whoever's behind the wheel.

"Drive," you say. "Drive and don't you dare stop."

Along the way, the driver starts talking every now and again, but you can hardly hear her. All you can hear, all you can see, is this great white fuzz whirring endlessly, repeating itself over and over.

YouLeftAlejandro'sFingersInNaomi'sFreezer AndShe'sGonnaFindThemSheHasFoundThemShe HasFoundThemAndShe'sGonnaKnowWhatYou DidYouMurdererYouMurderer YOU MURDERER.

YouMurderedAlejandroAndYouThoughtYou CouldGetAwayWithItYouThoughtYouCould IgnoreYourImpuritiesAndYouThoughtYou CouldLoveYourselfButYouCan'tYouCan't YOU CAN'T.

BecauseWhoCouldEverLoveAMurdererWho CouldEverLoveABadFriendWhoCouldEver LoveAPersonWhoRunsAwayFromResolutions AndHelpAndLove WHO COULD EVER LOVE SOMEONE WHO RUNS AWAY FROM LOVE???

HuhPhooHuhPhoo...

HuhPhoo...

HuhPhoo...

You pant and you gulp and you gasp. The white fuzz, white blur, THERE'S SO MUCH,

So much...

So much...

SO MUCH...

HuhPhoo...

It's too hard to breathe, it's too... IT'S TOO HARD...

Who could ever love someone who runs away from love?

HuhPhooHuhPhoo...

YOU MURDERER

YOU MURDERER

YOU MURDERER

YOU MURDERED ALEJANDRO

IT'S TOO HARD TO BREATHE

YOU CAN'T YOU CAN'T YOU CAN'T

SO MUCH WHITE FUZZ...

HuhPhoo...

YOU CAN'T BREATHE. She's Gonna Find Them She Has Found Them She Has Found Them.

I CAN'T BREATHE.

The car stops.

No no no, the car cannot stop, the car can never stop, not until you are in front of Naomi's house. The driver has turned around in her seat, she's peering at you, lines of worry scratched into her forehead.

"Are you okay?" she asks, almost fearfully.

"Yes. I'm fine. Please can you just keep driving?"

You avoid eye contact, staring at your knees, waiting desperately for the car to start moving.

"Are you sure you're okay? You seem a bit… panicked."

"I'm just in a hurry," you spit, your legs anxiously shaking up and down.

"You sure you don't wanna talk about anything?" She looks you up and down. "You can tell me anything. I won't tell anyone!"

"Really, please, I'm fine. The best help you can give right now is to drive."

The lady shrugs. "Okie dokie. But feel free to just blurt anything out at any time, it sure looks like it would do you some good."

You're still staring at your knees. *Shake shake shake* go your legs. The lady turns back around and the car rolls back onto the road. Don't listen to the white fuzz, don't look at it. Force your mind to be blank.

Oh, it hurts!

You strain and you strain and you strain. Oh, the throbbing pain.

Be blank.

You are blank.

In Waikiki, the driver asks where it is exactly you want to go. You don't dare tell her Naomi's address. Instead, you tell her the address of a house a couple streets away, where you get out and mutter a few inaudible words of appreciation. When you're sure she's well and truly driven away, you hasten to Naomi's house.

Standing on the footpath in front of the gate, the house lights are off. A breath of relief. And another, and another. You walk yourself across the front yard, onto the porch, to the doorstep.

You knock, paranoia thick in your throat. No response. You knock again. Silence. Silence. You pull the key out of your bra, turn it in the lock, swing the door open. Peering in, everything looks exactly as you left it. Naomi must still be in New York. Oh, the bliss of the fact! The bliss, the bliss, the bliss! You march over to the kitchen and yank open the freezer. The fingers! There they are, wrapped in foil, in all their vile glory. You loathe them, you want them. The relief of their presence is making you light-headed. You pull them out of the freezer tentatively, hoping the foil doesn't unfold. As soon as you are holding onto them you want to be rid of them. The cold of the foil against your sweaty palms makes the bile in your stomach curdle. You gag, hacking gags like

H

ACKSPLUT

TERWHE

EZE.

Saliva hangs from the edge of your chin. Don't drop Alejandro's fingers. Just leave now. Get out. Stop loitering in the vicinity of your very own death.

Out!

❧   ❧   ❧

You wish the mirror you are standing before is lying, you wish it were a deceitful bastard just like yourself. The pupils of your eyes are full stops. Your irises have faded almost to a cloudy grey, with an underwhelming tempest brewing beneath them. Your skin is muddy, thick with oil. Lines of self-pity are traced across your forehead, deep and stubborn. You are ugly. But it is the biggest truth you have seen since... well, you can't remember. You poor thing, you are so weak. You couldn't even bring yourself to stay away from this house, this house that overflows with putrid sadness. I am so sorry. You look so worn, so frayed. What did you do wrong? You've allowed your pupils to grow so small that you might lose them in the storm. You might blind yourself. Maybe it wouldn't be so bad to be blind if this is the only reflection you will ever see. Your grey eyes and your pasty skin and your bleached hair, it's washed you completely out, so much that you look like a ghost.

You are a phantom. A myth. A legend.

Maybe you should blind yourself and fall into a black abyss.

Maybe.

Look at your reflection.

Your ugliness is probably hurting the mirror. It might shatter soon. Let yourself fade, then. Let yourself fade into a grey smear.

A grey smear who once owned seven Chihuahuas.

A grey smear who has a loving father.

A grey smear who owns a black pearl.

Isn't the pearl supposed to heal you? Why aren't you healed?

You rub the pearl between your index finger and your thumb. Stale tears start melting into your fading face.

I want to be healed.

Mended, like an old piece of furniture that must be re-caned.

I want you to tape the petals back to the flower.

I want you to adjust the curly brass frame around your oozing brain.

I want you to punch that damn mirror, curse it for being so hostile.

Crack.

Now,

Cut yourself with a shard.

❧   ❧   ❧

You knock on the door of the Sunset Beach villa, again and again, clutching a bag of frozen human fingers. No one is answering. Donna-Maria is either asleep or gone. You are too tired to think what to do next so you continue to knock, listening to the monotony over and over like a lullaby. When your brain starts to numb and your knuckles ache, you climb through the bushes around the side of the house, spider webs catching in your hair. You stumble into the backyard, dust yourself off. At the foot of a mango tree, you kneel down and dig your hands into the pungent soil, crumbs of dark brown burrowing beneath your fingernails. And you dig. You dig until you have created a hole, a hole the size of a packet of frozen human fingers. You wedge the packet into the hole, shove it right down to the bottom, and you refill it. You pat the soil in place when you're done and step on it.

You sit on the front doorstep, waiting. You stare at a weedy flower just a couple of inches from your right foot. The key in your bra is digging into your breast. The flower doesn't move, neither do you. The sun comes up, goes down, comes back up again. You are waiting. Your muscles spasm and your neck jerks and acrid bile splashes from your lips. You wipe it away with the back of your hand. The key in your bra hurts so much that you can't feel it anymore, your throat is choked with phlegm. The dust on the road moves and you look up from the weed, look up at Donna-Maria. You stand up and hug her splintering frame. What an inadequate, futile hug. She opens the door and you follow her inside, leaving the weed by the doorstep to grow. Weeds are allowed to grow, too.

It's okay, weeds are allowed to grow.

And in the sunlight, they do.

᪥   ᪥   ᪥

You thoroughly abuse yourself with the sound of your own voice. You attack yourself, knife-like. The wounds make you feel numb. You don't stop the stabbing; ghosts can't stop stabbings. Ghosts just writhe in the anguish of their past. And when a hand reaches in to save you, you won't be able to hold onto it.

Donna-Maria bought you new bottles of shampoo and conditioner, the mini ones people take on vacations. They are scented lemon verbena. The first time you squeeze a blob into your hand, the smell is so startling that you find yourself stumbling into Winnie's house, knocking your head on the marble counters. There's Winnie, taking her lasagna out of the microwave, she sticks her finger into it and puts it back in the microwave. While her food heats up she disappears to her room and comes back with a bare face; her lips aren't shiny anymore. The microwave beeps, you jump, she takes the plate of lasagna out and sticks a fork in it. When she closes the cutlery drawer she looks up, looks around her beautiful kitchen, looks straight at you. Her smile is full of whiskey.

"I told you," she smiles, "you can't use my L'occitane lemon verbena body wash."

You start whimpering.

"I told you not to use it and you did. How could you do that to me? I thought you were my friend."

Whiskey is drooling down her chin and onto the slice of her lasagna. You yelp, the agony of the scene torturing you, feasting on you.

"HOW COULD YOU DO THAT TO ME?"

The wet tiles are harsh against your tailbone as you howl on the floor of the shower. You rock back and forth, hugging your knees as the water dribbles off your fingernails, howling, howling—

You are howling not like a lone wolf who howls to the beaming face of the moon, not like a baby who howls for the attention of his tired mother, not like a man who howls for the body of a curvy woman. You are howling like a girl who is both the wolf and the moon, the baby and the mother, the man and the woman. You are howling like a girl who is best friends with her greatest enemy. You are howling at yourself, you are a lone wolf, you are a silver moon.

But you thoroughly abuse yourself with the sound of your own howl. In summation, you are pathetic.

❧   ❧   ❧

You are sitting at the kitchen bench, picking grit from underneath your fingernails, contemplating what to eat next. Another mango or leftover Arancini balls? The mangos aren't as sweet anymore and the Arancini balls would be cold. Keep on picking at your pinkie, once it's clean then you can finally decide what to eat. A knock at the front door echoes through the villa, bounces off the beach wood. You look up from your fingers, listen intently to the proceeding silence. Another knock sounds throughout the house. You hear Donna-Maria's slipper-clad feet shuffling towards the door, dragging neatly across the floorboards. The sound of keys in a lock, the door clicking open. The muffled blurting of a girl's voice, the muffles sound like your name.

"*Confuso, confuso*," blabs Donna-Maria.

And then the girl's voice again, this time clearer: "A girl with pink hair? *Cheveux roses?*"

Your stomach wrenches itself apart.

"No... *confuso*," sighs Donna-Maria.

"Look," the girl huffs, "a girl with pink hair stole my credit card and did a bunch of other illegal *merde* and I need to know if you've seen her."

Cille.

It's Cille!

You cannot believe it.

You almost want to laugh, it's so hard to believe.

There is a silence that follows that is warped with Donna-Maria's confusion and Cille's impatience.

And then, "Ugh, okay, fine, I'll leave. Here's my number. Call me if you see her." The click of the door, the shuffling of Donna-Maria's feet. She comes to the kitchen and stares at you, questions pouring from her milky eyes.

But instead of answering any of them, you say, "I must go. I have to leave."

In your room, you snatch your tote bag, don't even bother looking what's inside it. At the bedroom window, you stick your finger in between the slats of the blinds and peep out to the road. There she is, there she *actually* is, walking with a straight posture, wheeling that tiny pretentious suitcase behind her, bumping unconventionally along the rubble. Never, never in a million years did you ever expect to see Cille lugging herself across the North Shore of Oahu for you. This time you let the laughter pour out of you, let it swirl around the room and pound against your ears. Look how scared you are. But there she is! Cille! Looking for you! You gotta go, you've gotta get out of here, you know that, right? Of course you know that—that's all you seem to know. You watch Cille until she disappears past the bend, feverishly impatient. Swinging your tote over your shoulder, you get out. Don't even say goodbye to Donna-Maria. Goodbye is for amateurs.

❧   ❧   ❧

You hitch a ride to the airport, oozing charm as always, such empty charm. At check-in, the lines are long, so you become a vendor of heavy sighs and sarcastic mutterings. When the agent finally sends you off with your boarding pass, you scurry off to security, struggling irritably to feign magnetism. You stick yourself on to the back of another line, impatience dripping from your temples.

"*Mon dieu!*" you hear from somewhere behind you, "can this line get any slower?"

The French, that vile French. You turn around and crane your neck, searching the line. And there she is. The one and only, Cille. You want to scream as loud as you possibly can, you want to rip holes through your very own eardrums. What is wrong with her? How dare she have the audacity to come here and present you with the very thing you ran away from.

"That bloody *connard*, putting me through all this bloody *merde*."

Her accent is stupidly perfect, just like her perfect education and her perfect bank account and her perfect knowledge of garnishes. It all just reminds you of how imperfect you are. It reminds you of Alejandro's six-month trip to the corner store, of the melancholic, dusty smell of second-hand book shops, and the absence of that exact same smell in libraries. It reminds you of Mrs. June's silver Subaru, of her too-frequent use of the word 'youngsters,' of Cravat's enraged phone calls. It reminds you of Winnie's marble benchtops and her capability to keep a job that you couldn't keep. It reminds you of fish and chips and iced lattes, of cats without opposable thumbs, of dry cereal, of platform espadrilles. It reminds you of your apartment's kitchen that bathes in sunlight and the pile of second-hand books skewed on the floor of your bedroom, of lime and ginger tea. It all just reminds you of home.

Home.

But is Bondi really home?

Or is it here, in Waikiki?

You're not entirely sure.

You don't belong anywhere, not really.

How traumatizing, how exhilarating.

You make sure Cille doesn't see you, discretely moving along with the queue.

Your hands are very clammy; you don't really belong anywhere.

You don't really belong to anything.

Or to anyone.

You're lost. Lost between acceptance and indifference, lost between hate and mediocrity. You are lost between the past and the present, confused as to which is which. You are lost between who you are and who you could be, wondering if who you are is all you will ever be. You want to be your favorite place, yet you are not whole enough to be a place; you are incomplete, a crumbling temple. You want to be a contradiction yet you don't want to be contradicted. Don't want to be conflicted. You don't want to be insane but you constantly get bored of sanity. You're lost, maybe because your life is complicated, or maybe it's just because you think too much about things. You want to be alone but you don't ever want to be lonely. You want to be the purest form of yourself by dousing yourself in your own fraudulence. You want to let people into your soul but only after they wipe their feet at the door. You want to reach into other people's souls but you can't even look them in the eyes. You want people to experience long, restless nights due to the thought of you; you want people to forget you ever existed. You miss yourself, you miss that little girl sitting on the wall by the beach with her mother, syrup dripping off her chin. She never picked flowers, just admired them with her curious eyes and nagged her sister to take photographs of them. She was indestructible, protected by a shiny film of innocence. You miss that little girl, you lost her, you fool. You thrust yourself onto a roller coaster of love and hate and passion and disgust in hopes of it taking you to a perfect version of yourself, unmarred by the flaws of your past and untouched by the infectious beauties of everyone else's lives. You failed though, failed miserably. The roller coaster just dumped you in a wretched heap, miles and miles away from sublimity. And now you are lost. You have no idea which direction to go, which path will take you to fulfillment. You don't know what to do, what to say, who to trust. You don't know who you are, let alone who you could be. You don't know if you love yourself or despise yourself. You don't know anything anymore. You don't know, you don't know, you don't know…

All you do know is you want a cup of lime and ginger tea, you want a gentle hug from your very own mother.

But most of all, you want to be engulfed by a great, black chasm.

You want to disappear.

Step 9

Become Temporary,
a Never-Ending Series
of Brief Interludes

THIS IS YOUR FIRST time in Noosa. Your attention isn't sharp enough to determine whether you like it here so far, but you haven't bumped into anyone who knows your name, so that's a good enough start. Looking down at a map printed onto the back of a brochure you picked up at the airport, you take yourself to a motel by the river in a section called Noosaville, and ask the receptionist for a room. She smiles and clicks away with her computer mouse, picks the mouse up and shakes it a couple of times, frowning, looks back at you, and grins. There's a bit of lipstick stuck on her front tooth, lipstick that matches the varnish on her clicking finger.

The receptionist peers over the rim of her tortoise shell glasses at the computer screen, continues clicking the damn mouse, and sighs softly every now and again, convincing you that she very nearly might've forgotten your presence.

Still looking at the computer, she asks, "How are you liking Noosa so far, sweetie?" *Click, click, click.*

"Fine, thanks."

"Have you been to the national park? What about Tea Tree Cove? It's gorgeous up there. Have you been shopping along Hastings Street? I could shop along there all day long; I swear, if you left me there for a couple of hours, I'd end up with an empty bank account and a declined debit card!"

You grunt, it was supposed to be a sort of laugh, but it hiccups out of you nevertheless. The receptionist peels her attention from the computer screen and looks to you, curious.

"I love your necklace. Aren't black pearls supposed to be rare? I love rare things. Where's that one from?"

"The Cook Islands."

"You've been to the Cook Islands?!"

"Uh-huh."

"I am so jealous. You sure do get around. What brings you to Noosa?"

You consider her question, irritated by the effort required to answer it, and then finally you remark, "So, how's that room coming along? It's okay if there isn't an availability, I'm sure I can find another place."

"Ah, yes! No! Don't leave, we have a room that's just opened up!" *Click, click, click.* "Why don't you follow me and I'll show you around the place? You'll love it."

The next thirty-seven minutes are unbearably vexing. The receptionist shows you around the whole motel, introducing you to the communal pool, the carpark, your room. She makes sure you like the smell of the set of mini shampoos in the bathroom and pulls the kettle out of a cabinet in the kitchen, because "people can never seem to find it, and so they leave without ever brewing themselves a cuppa!" Finally, after opening all the curtains and plumping all the pillows, the receptionist asks, "Do you have any questions?"

Yes, in fact, you do.

"Could I use a phone?"

"Why, of course! There's one right in reception."

"And could I quickly look something up on your computer?"

"Sure, I can take you back to the lobby."

Behind the desk, you type North Shore Oahu Real Estate, find their phone number and note it down on a pad of paper. You pick up the landline, dial the number, listen to the rings.

"*Aloha*, Hawaii Life Real Estate Brokers, this is Kenny speaking."

You proceed to give Kenny very detailed, very clear instructions. You tell Kenny to grab a pen and paper, to get ready to write down every word that he hears. You tell him that once you are done, he is to translate everything into Italian, everything. You tell him to write down exactly this:

Go into the bedroom. Under the bottom left corner of the mattress, you will find two hundred and fifty U.S. dollars. Take that money, go to Walmart and buy three of the cheapest suitcases you can find. Bring them back to the villa. If you don't spend all of the two hundred and fifty dollars, keep the change. Back in the bedroom, you can see piles of different sorts of things, like jewelery and cameras. Arrange everything into three even piles. Fill each suitcase with a pile. If anything doesn't fit, keep it. Now look under the other three corners of the mattress. Whatever you find there, distribute it evenly across the suitcases, except for one hundred and fifty U.S. dollars. Take the three suitcases and the one hundred and fifty dollars to the biggest post office on Oahu. Tell them you would like to mail the suitcases to the Sun Motel. The address is 265 Weyba Road, Noosaville, Queensland, Australia. The postcode is 4566. Tell them you would like express shipping. Pay with the one hundred and fifty dollars and keep any change for yourself. If you don't know how to say these things in English, or if you can't understand what the people at the post office are saying, refer to the glossary I attached for you. After they take the three suitcases, you can go back to your villa. Tidy up, do whatever you want, prepare for a new guest. I will not be coming back. Please do not try to contact me. Thank you for your help. Thank you for your generosity. Cille.

You make Kenny read it back to you, ensuring he has every single word. You tell him to get ready to write more. He is to find the Italian translation of:

Suitcase

I want to mail these three suitcases overseas.

I would like express shipping.

The address is 265 Weyba Road, Noosaville, Queensland, Australia. The postcode is 4566.

You tell Kenny to write out a sort of dictionary, each phrase in Italian followed by its English translation. He is to attach this to the previous message, which he must completely translate into Italian. Google Translate should do the trick for all of this. Once he has both the Italian paragraph and the glossary, he is to personally give these to Donna-Maria, one of the agency's clients. Do not e-mail it to her. Do not say it over the phone. Print it out and physically give it to her. You tell Kenny that you think you've covered everything. You ask him if he has any questions.

"I have a lot, actually."

"This is all government business, mind you, so I don't know how many of them I'll be able to answer."

You tell him that the only people that need to know about this phone call are him, you, and Donna-Maria. He understands. You ask him to run through everything you just told him, all the way from the beginning. It seems like he's comprehended your instructions thoroughly.

"Thank you, Kenny, that will be all."

You hang up. Fix the phone back in its socket on the wall.

"You're part of the *government!*" an excited voice hisses behind you, making you jump slightly. "Are you a secret agent? Or a spy? You must be a spy. That is so cool!" You turn around to the receptionist and smile tightly, her insisting excitement straining your nerves.

"Look, could you do me a favor? When three large parcels arrive, could you let me know?"

"Absolutely, ma'am. And don't you worry—I will keep my mouth sealed. Zip! Not a peep of this conversation will slip!"

You give her another tight, uncongenial smile before managing to slip away to your motel room.

In your room, you strip down and step into the shower, delighted to be washing away all the angst that had somehow accumulated in your pores over the last day or two. You let the water run icy cold, a bit like your feelings. You don't bother using the receptionist's carefully chosen shampoos and conditioners, they do nothing but scent your impurities rather than cleanse you of them. You turn the shower off and step onto the chipped tiles, not bothering to lay out a bath mat. You reach for a towel and wrap it loosely around your torso, tucking the corner so that it stays. Your reflection in the blemished mirror is demanding your attention. You give

it to her, reluctant. Her roots have grown back, a strip
of brown hair the color of dark chocolate, eighty-five
percent cacao. A striking contrast against the platinum
blonde. You should book an appointment with a
hairdresser—dispose of this contradiction promptly. A
girl cannot possibly feel found if she has two different
hair colors. The face of your reflection looks... worried.
Calm down. Don't fret. Fretting wastes time, wastes
intellect. Fretting will wrinkle your skin, will make you
look more like your mother.

Your mother.

Look, there she is, standing in the front yard, smelling
the frangipanis. Coughing, coughing so loudly that
the flowers wilted a little. You watched her from the
hammock. Watched her as she fished for her lighter
in the front pocket of her denim cut-offs. Watched
her curse as she couldn't find it. You, sixteen years old,
slipped your hand into your own pocket and wrapped
your fingers around the red BIC lighter, watched your
mother fiddle with an unlit cigarette. She turned around
and looked at you, morosely smiling, a world of worry and
brood dripping from the lines around that single grin.
She began walking over, her long brown hair swishing
softly. You watched your mother as she doubled over
and coughed maniacally. Watched as she dropped onto
her knees in the middle of the pretty garden. Watched
as she began dying in front of the marble statue of an
angel. You tumbled from the hammock. Panting. Your
head full of air. You felt defeat before being defeated.

On the grass you cradled you mother, held her head to your chest, smoothing her hair just like she used to smooth yours. On the grass, you cradled every single one of your fears, your fears that looked like a worn, beaten version of yourself, and you begged for them to stay with you. You begged her to stay with you. The smell of the jasmine was so overpowering that you began to cry.

"I'm going to call 911, okay, Mummy? You just stay right here, you hear me? I'll be right back."

You stood up and ran to the house. Behind you, you could hear your mother wheezing. Once you dialed 911, you listened to a woman's calm voice ask you what your emergency is. Standing on the wraparound porch, watching your mother die, you asked yourself what your emergency is.

"I don't have a dad that can help me," you told the calm voice.

"Do you have a mother?"

"No." It comes out as a whisper. "Not anymore."

"What happened? Miss, what is your emergency?"

"I don't have parents anymore. I only grew up with one, but then she turned into half of one. I hid her lighter from her to try and make her whole again. The doctors said drugs would fix her, but she didn't want drugs. She wanted her lighter. My emergency is that I'm abandoned. My dad abandoned me before he even knew me, and my mum, well, she decided to abandon me despite knowing me. I wasn't a very good reason for her to live, I guess."

Out in the middle of the yard, your mother had

completely stopped moving, her body curled amongst the grass, the angel statue watching over her. The scent of jasmine came with a rush of vertigo and was making you feel faint.

"Miss, what is your location?"

"I'm at home." But was it really home? No one who is abandoned truly has a home, not really.

"What is your address?"

"I don't have a home anymore."

You hung up.

You walked over to the frangipani tree, clutched onto its thin trunk, and shook it until the ground became a carpet of white and pink. You picked up a flower and brought it over to your mother, tucked the flower behind her ear. Oh, how she made death look so pretty.

Maybe that is why she chose death over you.

Maybe she'd rather be plucked for her beauty than admired from afar. Maybe she didn't want to be loved.

As if being loved were a burden.

A misfortune.

Your mother didn't love herself.

Oh, what a calamity.

❦   ❦   ❦

Someone is pounding against the door of your motel room. The word *Cille* starts throbbing in your head, an unpleasant pulse. She couldn't have possibly found you this fast, could she? The knocks resound once more, you recoil at the prospect of hearing French profanity. But instead you hear,

"Psssst! Secret agent! Your package has arrived! I repeat, your package has arrived!"

A surge of relief engulfs you. You unfurl your coiled chest and get up to open the door, the receptionist beaming feverishly on the other side.

"I was going to call the landline in your room instead of knocking, you know, just in case someone was watching, but then I thought: what if someone bugged the phone? So, I decided coming in person was a better option. See, I make a pretty good spy too, eh?"

You give her your best counterfeit laugh and follow her to the office. Sure enough, heaped in the corner are three large boxes, sent all the way from Hawaii. You rub your hands together, satisfied. Ripping open the boxes, you pull out the suitcases and prop them up on their wheels. "Will you help me bring them to my room?" you ask reluctantly.

"I would love to."

With a handle in each hand and the receptionist with one, you wheel the suitcases back to your room. After convincing the receptionist that you don't need her help to unzip them, she leaves you alone.

Donna-Maria has done a mighty fine job. Everything from your room is packaged neatly, the satin dresses folded in crisp lines and the passports stacked aptly. A mighty fine job, indeed. You take everything out, trying your best to preserve their pristine manor, and lay them out on the bed. It gives the motel room a certain opulence, one that you want to roll in. You then group everything into categories—clothes, jewelery, money, passports, cameras, miscellaneous. You cut the pile of money in half, putting the first half back in the suitcase and taking the second half to a currency exchange agency that you were given directions to by the receptionist. You return to the motel with a plenitude of Australian dollars.

You take one-quarter of the clothes, one camera, and one-third of the jewelery and put them in the suitcase with the foreign money. You take the remaining three-quarters of clothes, eight cameras, and two-thirds of jewelery to a pawn shop, the directions once again given to you by the receptionist.

"All of these items have been given to me by very, very rich people who simply got bored of everything," you tell the sweaty man behind the counter. "It's all awfully valuable."

The man grunts and scratches at his beard, unconvinced.

"You see this dress here? It's one hundred percent authentic silk, you can tell by its weight, see?" You hand him the dress and he holds it by the straps, letting the soft fabric tumble down. Another grunt gurgles from beneath his wiry moustache.

"All the cameras work, too. Try them! The jewelery isn't plated crap, I can assure you. One hundred percent sterling silver and gold. All the stones and stuff are real, too. Got all kinds of spiritual powers and deep meanings, you know, the type of stuff that makes rich people feel cultured. I'm telling you, all of this stuff is worth thousands."

The man pokes his fingers through a couple more things, then finally grunts when he makes a decision. "I'll give you a thousand."

"A thousand? Sir, with all due respect, one thousand dollars is what I'd expect for this single ring." You pick up a silver band encrusted with tiny sparkling diamonds, a big red ruby sitting atop it proudly.

"Fine. Five thousand."

You pick up five more rings and adjust them so that they catch the light, charming him into considering a higher amount. "All the jewelery put together is worth no less than ten thousand, sir, I can assure you."

"Well, do you have a certificate of authentication?"

"No."

"Then you can't assure me."

"But I told you," you huff, "these things were given to me as an act of plain impulse. They were owned by people whose underpants are more expensive than all these cameras put together."

Yet another grunt gurgles from his beard. "Five and a half."

"Ten thousand. Please."

"Six."

"Deal."

Grunt.

Back at the motel, you're not entirely sure what to

do with all the passports. When you took them from the resort, you made sure to only take the ones that even slightly resemble you, ones that presented a vague connection between you and the passport owner, a false connection, but a connection nonetheless. But looking at them now, all the platinum blonde heads and olive-brown skin, it feels wrong somehow. You don't want the help of these people to assist you in disappearing. You don't need their help, either. By taking these passports, you made connections.

Connection is the inverse of disappearance.

That can only mean that connection is the inverse of finding yourself. Connection is permanence, an anchor.

Connection is forgetting to admire the flower.

Forgetting the flower is even there.

Disconnect.

You borrow a pair of scissors from the receptionist. With them, you cut the passports into strips, turning identities into confetti. Back to the receptionist, return the scissors, inquire about an oven. She tells you that you can use hers. You're in her car now, clutching a plastic bag filled with confetti, listening to her talk back to the radio. At her house, she takes you to the kitchen. You ask if you can have some privacy, you know, top-secret government stuff. When she leaves, you find a baking tray in one of the cabinets, sprinkle it with the confetti, and crank the oven up to the highest temperature. You slot the baking tray into the oven, take a seat at the kitchen bench, and wait. You wait, and you wait, and you

wait. Not for minutes, not for hours, but for a collection
of moments, sitting in a pool of consciousness. Time is
fictitious. The confetti is completely black now, so you
turn off the oven and take out the tray. Hot air kisses
your face. The smell of charcoal is tall and aggressive.
Wrapping your fingers in wads of paper towel, you crush
the blackened confetti until you are left with a tray of
ashen powder. You pour it into the sink, turn on the tap,
and watch it wash down the drain, wash your hands,
too. The kitchen smells a bit funky, but you're sure the
receptionist won't mind. After all, you are a secret agent
of the government, one who owns seven Chihuahuas
and has a musically talented boyfriend. You are anything
and everything.

❀   ❀   ❀

With everything you own in a single suitcase, you check
out of the Sun Motel and check into a hotel on the
other side of Noosa, by the coves. It has dry-cleaned
bed sheets and a Dyson hairdryer. Nobody talks to
you, you don't talk to anyone, a reciprocation of energy.
By day, you are a pool-dweller, dipping in and out of
chlorinated water that sparkles almost as much as the
jewelery dripping from your limbs. By night, you are a
gelato connoisseur, your tongue becoming an expert of
twenty-four artisanal flavors. Six of them are sorbets.
When you get bored, you pack up your things and rent
a holiday house tucked into the national park. You go

on hikes and swat mosquitoes. For six nights in a row you have a grilled cheese for dinner. Lindt chocolate for dessert. When you can't figure out the washing machine, and you're in rather desperate need of one, you take off and settle into a resort right on the sand of Noosa's main beach. You have facial massages and wander up and down Hastings Street, buying sun hats and acai bowls. You re-dye your hair, get it layered, too. Stuff everything back into your suitcase—it's harder to close now, what, with all that shopping.

After wandering around for a while, wheeling the suitcase behind you and admiring your hair in the reflection of car windows parked next to the footpath, you come across a brothel. You walk inside, just for fun. You look through a catalogue of sculptural men, just for fun. You book a room, just for fun. A charming smile is plastered on your face. At dusk, gospel music floats into your room from the church two doors down, and when there's a knock at your door you ignore it just so you can listen to the music for a little while longer. Through the wooden slats covering the single small window, you can see plumes of pink clouds, rosy foam on a pint of beer, and the ecclesiastical melody spins them into cotton-candy. You don't end up answering the door. Instead, you drink the beer and eat the cotton-candy all by yourself. It is a night of self-indulgence.

After the brothel comes another motel, a bed-and-breakfast cottage, a backpacker's lodge, a beachside retreat, and two hotels, but you didn't even manage to sleep overnight in one of them after finding bloodstains on the carpet. Now, sitting in an armchair in your room at the Tea Tree Hotel and Day Spa, you're not quite sure what to do with yourself. You don't want to waste your precious youth sitting in this scratchy armchair, yet you don't really fancy getting out of it anytime soon.

You are alone. You are surrounded by things that don't matter. You're not being judged by anyone or anything. You have the time, and the space, to do anything.

Isn't this what you wanted?

Sitting here, the scratching fabric irritating your upper thighs, you can almost try and convince yourself you're sitting in the Bondi public library hunched over a yellow-paged paperback. You can feel the absence of the melancholic, dusty smell of second-hand bookshops, you can even feel the warmth of knowing that your three favorite smells are lavender, lemon verbena, and second-hand bookshops. You can feel the satisfaction of having to do without that smell, having to do without magic. Sitting in this itchy armchair, you know you are both the protagonist and the antagonist, just like the sun.

You are just like the sun.

The funny thing is, this itchy chair, this tiny splinter of your past, is comforting to you.

The thought of your past is a comfort.

Say that again, I dare you.

The thought of your past is a comfort.

There are three figures sitting on the floor before you, legs crossed and eyes round like eager kindergarten students. The first one you immediately recognize as Winnie. Her smile, as always, is full of whiskey, framed by a smothering of coral lip gloss. When you identify the second figure, your stomach twists gruesomely and a hot flush creeps up the back of your neck. Damn Alejandro. That beautiful boy, a hole below the neckline of his T-shirt, which has been washed in fabric softener. A dark brown curl falls in front of his eye, and with a twitch of his head, he flicks it back. You want to reach out and slap him, you hate him so much. You want to lean in and kiss him, you love him so much. When you look at the third figure, you do a double take. You rub your eyes, plagued with disbelief, but when you look up again she's still there. Jesus Christ, it's really Mummy. A waterfall of shiny brown hair, a cigarette clinging from her lower lip, mischief and sadness etched into her face like a sculpture. My darling mummy is here! Your whole past is here. Look at it.

Look at your past.

Look at your first day of school in Australia, all the tenth graders assessing you with their beady eyes, a girl with an infectious smile offering you a purple pen that she got for free.

That time when you both lounged at the rock-pools by the beach like lizards, chewing on candy bracelets, tanning your bare backs and talking about boys.

Look at your past.

Look at your third shift at The Orchard, you served a Spanish boy, and he told you he was a gentleman, you told him to prove it. He said he'd take you to a matinee the next morning, his accent curling luxuriously. That matinee was so good you went to the same show that same night, with that same Spanish boy.

That time when you both sat cross-legged on the living room floor of your apartment, indulging in staring contests and eating mint ice cream straight from the tub, drinking too many cans of flat beer.

Look at your past.

Look at the woman who challenged you to a hula-hoop contest the night before your math exam, in which you were boldly defeated. You collapsed on the grass, giggling because you couldn't believe Mummy beat you.

That time when she sang a soft Hawaiian lullaby while you cried and cried, your tears muddying in her smooth hair, the closest thing you've ever heard to the voice of an angel.

Look at your past.

Look at you curled in your single bed beneath your lacy duvet, sleep a foreign concept, the room dusty with darkness. You can feel the void in your mother's room, her empty bed, the sheets unmade. You can hear Naomi's muffled sobs, sitting in the rickety chair by your vanity, waiting for you to fall asleep. Pointless, really. You sit up, tell Naomi that you can't sleep if she keeps crying. She tells you she'll go back to her room then, *I'm sorry, I'll go back to my room*. You told her, no. You told her, you'll go. You'll go somewhere, anywhere, as long as it is away from this boundless suffering. She tells you not to be ridiculous, fall asleep. But you can't stop thinking about the unmade bed and the red BIC lighter and the photographs in the safe. You get out of bed, Naomi stands up. You tell her you want to live with Aunty, in Austria. She tells you she doesn't even live in Austria, she lives in Australia, idiot. You don't mind, you'll just live in Australia. Anything is better than this tragedy. Naomi cries some more, even though she's supposed to be the bigger sister, the brave one. What a stupid excuse for reality it all was.

That was the first time you decided to disdain the very thought of your past, to suppress the mere essence of it.

That was the first time you hated yourself.

The ghosts of your past are right here in front of you. You could touch them if you really wanted to...

Kiss them, even.

But you just look at them,

Serene,

Not scared.

You are not scared to become acquainted with ghosts of your past.

Become friends, even.

Your past is a comfort to you. Let it haunt you.

❧ ❧ ❧

Check out of the hotel, try to find a bus stop. Strolling down the street is too much work in this heat; the footpath is a dripping mirage of sweat, making your hair damp. You keep having to lick the sweat off your upper lip. As you walk past a strip of stores, the relieving flush of air-con greets you, so you stop for a moment just to let your clothes dry a little. The air-con, it seems, is coming from a flower shop. Not a florist, but the type of shop you'd hope you will frequent when your hair is grey and your favorite pastime is pruning. You walk in, just for a brief stop-over, and browse, sticking your nose into pollen and petting kitsch garden gnomes, your suitcase rolling behind you. You circle the entire shop two or three times, each time your attention wandering back to a plastic pot filled with a gorgeous abundance of cotton-candy-pink geraniums. They are luminous in the sunlight. The sight of it is too tempting to ignore any longer, so you pick it up and take it to the cash register, careful to not touch the petals.

You once heard that if you touch the petals of a flower they wilt faster.

You pay seventeen dollars; the pot is all yours.

You continue walking until you finally find a bus stop, sunshine glaring. You take a seat on the silver bench that's too hot to sit on comfortably, your suitcase propped beside your feet, your flower pot nestled next to your right hip. You sit there for a little while, numbly counting the number of people who walk past, wondering if you should ask one of them if they have a bottle of cold water they wouldn't mind sharing.

A short woman with perfect circles of grey hair wobbles past you, noisy red shoes loose enough at the heels to give them tender blisters. When she's a couple of paces away, something falls from her handbag, and without really thinking, you pop up from the bench and rush to retrieve it. When you bend down, you see a gorgeous pair of harlequin sunglasses, the frames a glassy black with curly custard detailing on the outer corners. They would suit you, don't you think? You look back up to see if the lady has noticed, but she's become a stout blur in the distance. So, you pick up the glasses and take them with you back to the bench. You put them on, slide them up the bridge of your nose. Now the sun isn't so bright.

A bus pulls up in front of you and a couple passengers step out. Before you is an advertisement plastered to the bus window, an advertisement for a travel agency. There is a smiling flight attendant and a list of four discounted flights: Sydney, New York, Hawaii, Europe.

You remember when you became an unemployed burden in Bondi. An inbox of half-opened e-mails, an apartment filled with yellow books and grey memories, and you. Very selfish, very lonely, very confused between what you were running away from and what you were running to. You don't blame her for everything she did wrong, she was just trying to fix herself. You wonder if she did a good job of it.

You remember when you became an elite con-artist in New York. Seven Chihuahuas became your best friends and piano notes were the only sound that could drown out the rage of bees that buzzed inside of you. It is easy to learn to steal when your heart has already been stolen. That much you have learned.

You remember when you became a murderer in Hawaii. A murderer. You became a *murderer*. You murdered a real-life person, a real memory, a real part of your life.

Alejandro?

Alejandro???

God, you miss him.

What have you done! Don't you dare start crying—stop that! Stop it. Stop *crying*. Answer me! What have you done? Look what you've done. Oh, God, you hated yourself so much, didn't you? You created a ghost just so that it could haunt you. You dug your own grave that day and tried to bury yourself in it. You *hated* yourself *so* much.

Please, don't hate yourself anymore. It hurts too much.

You are startled by a voice that is coming from somewhere nearby.

"The sight of good flights makes you cry tears of joy, eh? Me, too." A man in a wrinkly suit is setting his briefcase onto the other side of the bench. "That Europe one sounds especially good."

You glance at him and smile a little. The bus's engine starts up, and as it pulls away, you watch your reflection flicker in the moving windows. The top half of your hair is deep brown and the bottom almost white. The stolen glasses hide your puffy eyes quite well, but you can still see them, just slightly. You have a glacé-cherry nose from being in the sun too long. You look very small, almost tiny, and you want to leap forward and give yourself a hug, kill your enemy with kindness. The pink flowers are a little wilted. Their petals wave at their reflection shyly.

"You know," you start saying, to the flowers, perhaps, though you can't be sure, "I've had some issues with my past self, but she was young, and I think I can forgive her."

The flowers wait patiently for you to continue.

"I'm not saying I'm perfect, or anything pretentious like that… I know that I have a strong tendency to digress and my sarcasm is better than my manners. I know that I'm awkward and bitter and hopelessly confused, I know all that. I know that I compulsively pick flowers rather than appreciate them, but I promise I'll appreciate you, I promise. You know, I'm not entirely sure why I pick the flowers… I think it's because I hate the idea that they could be better than me, that they *are* better than me." You chuckle slightly, disappointedly amused by the words coming out your mouth. "I think I might be scared of not being good enough. I wasn't good enough for my dad to stick around, and then I wasn't good enough for my mum to stick around, either. And Alejandro, he took off for six months—I wasn't a good enough reason for him to stay. I wasn't a good enough friend—Cille was robbed and Winnie was murdered. I was never a permanent source of happiness for anyone. But you know, now that I think about it, maybe that's because I'm not a permanent source of happiness for myself. And that's bad, I think, because happiness is key, both long-term and short-term, happiness is always key."

You and the pot plant sit in silence for a few moments, letting your thoughts settle into some sort of comprehensible picture.

"I won't pluck you," you tell the flowers, "I promise, I know I won't. You wanna know how I know? Because now I know that I *am* enough. I know that I am more than my pain. I am the sun and you need me to grow—I am necessary. I have always been enough. Always have been, always will be."

A light breeze flirts with the pink flower petals, a pink that reminds you of your once-upon-a-time cotton-candy hair. You ask the man with the wrinkly suit where the closest park is.

"Keep walking right down the end of this street, turn right, take the second left, and it's at the very end of that road. There's a pond and a swing set. I used to take my nephew there."

"Oh good, thanks. Have a good day."

"Yes, you too. Maybe I'll see you on a flight to Spain one day, eh? Imagine that!"

You follow the man's instructions fairly easily, suitcase in one hand and flowers in the other, and soon enough you find the park. You gaze over it for a few moments, and decide on a soft-looking patch just below an old magnolia tree. You get onto your knees and start digging. After a while, with soil smudged into the sweat in your hairline, you have a hole big enough for your flowers. You carefully remove them from the plastic pot and replace them into the hole.

Refilling it with soil, you pat and pat until they're standing proudly and sweetly in the magnolia's shade. You stand up, take a couple of steps back, and admire what you have just done.

You have freed the flowers and given them room to grow.

You have never been more peaceful than you are right now, your life packed neatly in a suitcase, the shade not too cold, the sun not too glary. Everything is just right, not perfect, but just right.

Just like you.

Just like me.

Just like us.

We are enough.

Step 10

Be Absolutely,
Positively Certain.

*(Although I Do Admit, If You've Gotten This Far,
Then It Is Already Too Late To Change Your Mind.)*

YOUR MIND IS A painting, and it looks like this:
The vices and virtues of
Kindness
(or is it love?)
Your teeth sink into a Portuguese tart, your twelfth
one of the week, and your body sways with the gentle
cadence of the ferry. The tart is devoured in three quick
bites. You open a bottle of water, take a swig, hope that
your pink geraniums are getting watered regularly.

You unzip your suitcase and pull out a notebook you
took two days ago at a market in Lagos. It was poking

out of the pocket of a slender woman's nice corduroy
jacket. It is no bigger than your hand, bound in faded red
cloth, the front embellished with a tiny gold heart.

In fractured Portuguese, you ask the person next to you
for a pen. He fishes around in his backpack, offers it to
you with a satisfied grin. Upon opening the notebook,
you discover that the slender woman has already found
solace in confiding in it. The first few pages are adorned
with rushed handwriting, the text interspersed with
doodles. You put down the pen, squint your eyes. Written
on the inside of the front cover is '*To Catarina, with all my
love, Arturo.*' You gently run your fingers over the looping
letters, imagine for a few fleeting moments that you are
the adored Catarina, realize that maybe you are Arturo
and Catarina all at the same time. You continue reading.
At the top of the first page in big, swirly letters is inscribed,
'*All the Things That I Know for Sure.*' Underneath is a list:

- No one is unlovable, some are just unloving.
- The pit of self-loathing is bottomless.
- Death is not an event, it is a place suspended
between memory and imagination.
- Everyone is scared, and everyone checks
their reflection in the windows of parked cars.
Sometimes the latter is a result of the former.
- Aliens are real.
- Everything that is authentic is also a paradox.
For example—Life, because it is inevitably
accompanied by death. Happiness, because it is

inevitably followed by sadness (life happens in
seasons, emotions are cyclical). Etc.
• Coffee will always taste better in a takeaway cup.
• Morals are malleable, not transformable.
• The past is never dead—it hasn't even passed.
• Happiness is key.
• No one should ever slow-dance in the dark.
• One must always water their flowers. The only
reason the grass looks greener on the other side
is because if one is constantly looking at someone
else's garden, they neglect their own.
• The greatest song of all time is "The Girl from
Ipanema" by Stan Getz, João Gilberto, and Astrud
Gilberto.

You are decidedly fond of this list; it's making you
smile gently. It feels nice, feels real. You read it over
again, sewing it into your soggy pink brains. It is the
first concrete, unchangeable thing you have known, and
held, in a while. Turn the page, find a shopping list.

eggs
unsalted butter
blueberry yogurt
coconut chips
sweet potato
rice
tomatoes
polenta

ricotta
chocolate wafers
muesli
frozen pizza
something to make the hydrangeas grow better
(fertilizer??)

Turn the page, feel a stare searing into the top of your head, look up. In the seat in front of you a man is slouched, the cuff of his black skinny jeans millimeters away from the toe of your flats. He takes a comb out of his pocket, runs it through his gelled hair, and winks. You continue to stare at him, wondrously amused. He slides the comb back into his pocket and retrieves a pack of gum. He unwraps a piece, a thick silver ring with an imprint of the Playboy bunny choking his index finger. Pops the piece in his mouth, chews and smiles, smiles and chews. He leans forward, offers you a piece. His breath smells of booze and roses, peppermint lingering on his fingertips. You take it, unwrap it, chew and smile, smile and chew. You blow a bubble and the sound of the pop makes the man twitch excitedly. He sits up now, adjusts the collar of his leather jacket, brings his right ankle to the top of his left thigh.

"Your parents sure did a fine job," he chews.

"How do you know that?" You sew a thick accent into your words, New Yorker.

"Well, pretty lady, any pair o' parents would be mighty proud of a specimen such as yourself."

You laugh, throw your head back a little, roll your eyes.

"I think you got it all wrong."

"How so?"

"Well, my father didn't want anything to do with my life, and my mother chose death over staying with me."

"Oh."

"And anyways, I don't really wanna make them proud."

"Oh."

He takes his comb back out of his pocket, pushes it through his hair again for good measure. His right foot gently starts bouncing up and down, up down chew, up down chew. You watch it over and over.

"I'd like to make *myself* proud, though."

You watch the bouncing get faster.

"Yeah?"

"Yeah. That would be the greatest success of all." You flick him the wrapper of your gum.

For the rest of the ferry ride, you watch the man writhe.

When the ferry gets to Morocco, you stay in your seat, wondering if anyone has stopped to look at the geraniums yet. You are hurriedly writing in your new notebook—there is no need to get off this ferry and see the world if the world has been you all along. So, stay here and keep writing:

Two months ago, I saw my face on a poster. For a brief moment, I didn't recognize myself. Anybody who watched the scene play out might've concluded that what they saw was Jay Gatsby peering at a poster of James Gatz. I inspected the cotton-candy pink of her hair, her short eyelashes and freckled nose. I hated how the girl staring back at me from that poster recognized herself in me—it made me want to tear it off the telegraph pole. In the end, I didn't bother mulling over the peculiar thing for too long, because the message the poster was entailing was completely wrong, and I ought to slap the daft bastard who made it. Above the picture of my face was the word 'MISSING.' The bloody fools... I am not missing, *I am found! I found myself! Like a little girl searching for treasure, I dug as deep as possible, right into the dark corners of my greying, murderous carcass, and I found the treasure under a pool of tears and sorrow and guilt. Imagine if the poster were actually correct: it would have the word 'FOUND' in golden, swirly letters, and underneath it would be a photograph of pink geraniums tucked into the soil beneath a magnolia tree.*

The ferry's horn blares like a song and you are once again dancing with the Mediterranean tide. You continue documenting the happenings of the past few months—your mind is a painting, ever changing, it seems, and it looks like this:

A disappearance, almost like a magic trick.

Four thousand dollars.

A coat that smells of dusty linen and expired dreams.

Hair dyed black, like the fur of a witch's cat.

A coffee-less coffee machine

Accompanied by lipstick the color of red wine.

Various hearts, most of them broken, if not all.

Aquatic Pilates and a family photo of Chihuahuas.

A bicycle. A body. A brain, oozing.

Platinum blonde, a tacky hair color.

So much love. So much hate.

Thick folds of jewels and silk, stamped pages and thick lenses.

Maybe a mended heart…

Maybe.

You wonder, if such a painting were to be displayed in a gallery, if people would stop to look at it. Nudge their friend, offer a vague nod to the direction of the picture so that both the person and the friend are stopping and looking. You'd like to think one of them would take a picture of the painting, perhaps on their phone, or on a disposable camera, and they might show it to another friend who didn't have the privilege of seeing it in person, or stick it on their wall with double-sided sticky tape so that they can look at it again, and again, and maybe again.

Eh, who are you kidding?

Nobody would stop to look at a few muddy smudges that are much too incomprehensible to be enjoyed, much too abstract.

But then again, such an outcome is expected of such a painting designed for such an acquired taste.

That acquired taste, of course, being yours.

That acquired taste, of course, deriving from you.

You're the only person who needs to like the painting, just like you're the only person who needs to water the pot of geraniums.

Chin up, my darling, don't be so cynical about such an

abstract picture. After all, if one were to translate it, if one were to read it as if it were a hieroglyph, they would find that it would say, 'you.'

They would be looking at you.

❦ ❦ ❦

You find yourself standing in Spain, and the chime of Alejandro's accent is pulsing through your arms and tingling your fingertips. An orange sign says '¡*Bienvenido a Algeciras*!' You are surrounded by seas of people, yet you manage to stay afloat, like a slice of lemon in a glass of water. You walk, because that is the only thing you are absolutely certain you know how to do without asking for help, you walk on and on and on, so that it feels like forever. In a strange sort of way, you will walk for the rest of your life. Suitcase in one hand, harlequin sunglasses hanging from the other, you will walk until you die, and when the highway ends you will have to find another one. The only time you will stop is to rest, like a gardener after she's watered her roses.

On the side of the road, you see a cemetery, its grey tombstones protruding from the hill like the flailing hands of the dead. You veer off the main road, your suitcase trundling through the uncut grass, and pass through the knee-high curly iron gates. The sun is beaming, entirely oblivious of the writhing souls beneath the soil. You let go of your suitcase by the gate and balance the glasses on top of it.

Graveyards are museums. The first time you visited the tombstone of your mother, when you were sixteen, you read the stone like an information plaque and wondered about the artifact's life. You had pretended to be the museum guide.

"This is the resting place of Denise Hale," you had whispered to the rest of the artifacts on display. "She was a mother of two, and the possession of no one. She did a lot of smoking, and had a lot of cancer, and has a lot of things to say sorry about. She was different, because she was a good mother and a bad mother all at once, but I loved her, and I think she loved me, so I guess it was okay for her to be different. Her greatest accomplishment in life was her ability to be herself even when she could be anyone else. I don't know many people who do that."

You only ever visited that museum once.

At this museum, you slowly take in each of the displays, reading the names in your head and making up a life for them. Luis Alcaraz, who lived for eighty-nine years, would have been a lighthouse keeper, looking over Arturo and Catalina, making sure their ships never sank. Angelina De Valle, dead at the age of seventy-two, would have been an opera singer, making seas of crowds cry and flirting with the conductor of the orchestra. Alejandro Escamilla. Died at the age of twenty-one. He would have smelled like fabric softener. An abundant bank account. A sparse wardrobe. He would have been killed by the malice of a lost little girl.

A couple of rows away, a little girl and her father are kneeling solemnly by a headstone. The girl reaches forward and pets it lovingly whilst the father wipes tears from her soft, round cheeks. You stroll over and watch them a little closer. The little girl turns to her father, leans in close, and whispers something. He nods, runs his hand through her hair, and begins to fiddle with something at the back of her neck. He retrieves a tiny gold necklace, the chain glinting in the sun. The girl grabs it with her tiny fist, turns back to the headstone, and lays it carefully over the top. They both get up of their knees, collect their things, and walk away.

You walk up to the headstone, pick up the necklace and inspect it. The gold is flawless. You slip it into your pocket.

You begin to observe the rest of the mourners. An old lady with a walking stick, who looks as if she has stood in front of that headstone a thousand times before, crosses herself and mumbles, "Amen." Two middle aged men cry hysterically at a headstone, their heads dipped and their shoulders trembling. A girl, no older than eighteen, sits cross-legged at the foot of a tombstone, staring into the middle distance.

From each of them, you steal a rosary of emerald beads, a battered wallet, and an embroidered handkerchief respectively. Who knew a nomadic thief could be so likeable.

You sit by a tomb and rest your head. Alejandro is just an artifact in a museum now, a piece of your history, just like your mother, just like Winnie, and just like you. The sooner you store your past in a mausoleum, the better. But it is okay. You can still pay your respects at the mausoleum. You can admire its stained-glass windows. You can always go back to the mausoleum and give thanks to the artifacts that showed you how to be you.

But you must not live inside the tomb.

❧ ❧ ❧

Your whole body is sore. Walking hurts. Your arm has gone numb from pulling the suitcase for so long, and the wheels are about to spin off any second, worn down from the gravel. You can't see anything for miles, just hills atop hills. You drop your suitcase onto the side of the road, sit on it, and fish out your little Portuguese notebook.

You write: *I am starving.*

You write: *I want to go home.*

You write: *But I am my home.*

You write: *Where's the kitchen?*

You close the notebook and stare at the desolate road. You can hear a car way off in the distance, the whir on the tarmac anticipating an exchange of presences. A blue Beetle manifests from heat waves and you watch it make its way along the road. As it gets closer to you, it slows down. You think, *oh, God, what have I done*, you think, *do I run or do I shout*, you think, *will this person snicker or swear?* You try to find a face beyond the tinted window, but fail. The car stops, the front door opens, a boot steps onto the tarmac. A curly French word floats from the car's interior. In all her irritating, obnoxious, successful glory, Cille stands in front of you. She is the crucifix at the front of the mausoleum.

"Come on," she says, "get in."

Without speaking, you get up, haul your suitcase into the trunk, buckle yourself into the passenger seat, stolen trinkets nestled in your lap.

"What's with the green beads?" she asks, snarky, superior, nodding at the rosary you're clutching.

"What's with the tone?"

"*Dieu*, I just saved you from the longest walk of your life. Be a little nicer, eh?" She starts the car and begins to drive.

"What are you doing in Spain?" you ask her, finally looking up at her face. She hasn't changed a single bit. She's still glorious, still perfect. She still knows the difference between parsley and coriander.

"Looking for you, of course."

You stop looking at her. Glare at the road ahead.

"Why would you want to do that?"

"Well," she sighs, her gaze fixed on the same view as yours, "I'm worried about you."

"Oh please, you don't need to waste your time worrying about me."

She stops the car.

"Shut up."

"I beg your pardon?"

"Ever since the day you dropped out of uni I have been worried about you. Your friend Winnie didn't stop crying, and Alejandro didn't stop punching walls, and your aunt called the police. And they traced you to New York but you disappeared again, and then Winnie disappeared and I thought, oh, maybe she found her, but then Alejandro disappeared and I was so worried, and suddenly I remembered you are Hawaiian, so I booked the next flight to Waikiki and I looked everywhere, and I asked everyone, and I followed the tiny traces of you that I managed to find all the way to here, in this crummy city on this crummy road with some crummy souvenirs."

The car is static with silence.

Fuzzy and warm.

"Why were you so worried?"

She looks at you as if you asked the color of the sky.

"Because you are my friend and I love you. Is it such a crime to worry about the people I love?"

You turn on the static again.

You had never considered this.

You had never opened your eyes wide enough.

God, you idiot!

You are loved!

You are loved, you are loved, you are loved.

I love you.

She loves you.

We love you.

"Thank you," you tell her.

"That's okay, *idiote*. Where do you want to go?"

"Anywhere."

Cille starts the car again.

"By the way, I like your souvenirs. They're unique. Just like you."

You look down at them and think that she's right, they are unique, and they are a testament to your refined skills. They are a souvenir not of your morals but of your potential. Maybe Cille would be comforted by a souvenir like that, seeing as she's your friend, your true friend.

"They're for you."

"But I don't need a handkerchief."

No, but she needs to know that she has a friend.

❦   ❦   ❦

By the time the sun is asleep Cille still hasn't driven anywhere worth stopping at, so she pulls into a motel and orders you both a bowl of rice and beans. Through this you find out that, of course, she can speak basic Spanish. You sit cross-legged on the bed and eat in tired silence. You want to be her. Yet you are so glad that you are you. Mother, how could you be yourself so seamlessly? You get up and drink a glass of water.

The following morning, you wake up while Cille is still engrossed in her beauty sleep. You are reminded of your sparse university days. You are at the mausoleum. You don't have to go inside, just peer through the tinted windows, like sun rays would. Remember I told you? You're just like the sun. You can see Cille buying you a cup of hot coffee in between classes, and picking your laundry up off the carpet. You can see her carefully analyzing the reference photos you collated when you decided you wanted to dye your hair a different color. She liked purple best. You chose pink. Looking through the stained-glass windows, you can see your friend Cille, pouring over columns of miniscule print, pages of newspaper splayed across the coffee table. Cille is very good at being herself. That must be why you are so jealous. Let's applaud her. She deserves recognition for her brave feat, just as you do. You find the nearest coffee shop and order a double espresso in a takeaway cup, no lid. It is made with a retro red coffee machine. You have the urge to steal the machine and gift it to Cille, but the barista is busy using it. Maybe there's one at the Duty-Free section of the airport. You bring the espresso back to the motel room with a copy of the local paper, wake her up gently, gather your belongings and leave.

"Where are we going?" asks Cille.

"To get sushi or commit a felony. I'll decide on the plane."

You ask the motel manager to call you a cab. You tell the driver to take you both to the closest airport.

You once again find yourself in a state of temporality, uprooted for the sake of discovery. At the airport, everybody belongs—it is your favorite place in the whole entire world. You sit and watch people chase happiness as if it is a destination. You want to speak into a loudspeaker and remind everyone that just because happiness is key does not mean there is a treasure chest that has to be unlocked.

In Duty-Free, whilst Cille is busy trying on watches, you search for a red coffee machine. You find it eventually, sparkly and cheaper than the one from Manhattan. You don't have a bag big enough to smuggle it away—they're all getting packed into an airplane. So, you take it to the checkout and pay for it. When Cille finds you, she smiles inquisitively at the big package you're cradling.

"What's the coffee machine for?"

"You."

She laughs, unsure of whether you are serious or not, but when you unload it into her arms she says, "You know you're crazy, right?"

You are uncomfortable accepting praise and tell her that you need to pee.

In the restrooms, you inspect yourself in the mirror. Your roots have completely grown back. You do not have the urge to uproot your geraniums. You recall the countless times you recolored your hair, as if the presence of its natural color was a chemical pesticide that stunted your growth. You realize now that the presence of your natural color proves that you were blooming all along—you just had to wait for spring to properly blossom. You turn on the faucet and wash your face, thinking how healthy and bright the geraniums must be with all that space to spread its roots. In the corner of the washroom, you sit on a lone stool and find your red notebook, flipping to a fresh page. At the top, in big capital letters, you write: HOW TO LOOK AFTER FLOWERS. Beneath, you write carefully...

Whatever you do with them, you must keep watering them. If you ever get tired of watering them, you can't just replace them with a bouquet of artificial flowers.

You have to persist.

Don't ever pluck a flower.

Don't ever let somebody else pluck a flower.

If they are interested in your pot of geraniums, tell them to look without touching. If they suggest putting them in a vase, inform them that they need soil for nutrients.

Give the flowers sunlight.

Please, remember that all flowers eventually die.

Please, remember that all flowers eventually blossom.

Please, remember that dying and blossoming are cyclical; one relies on the other.

Your mind is a painting, and therefore you are in an art gallery. A lady washes her hands and smiles at you in the mirror.

Your flight is called over the speakers.

You walk down the gangway next to Cille.

You are ready for take-off.

Acknowledgments

FIRST AND FOREMOST, I would like to thank Eddie Vincent, Michael Piekny, Deirdre Wait, and the entire team at Encircle for believing in me despite my inexperience, and providing me with this opportunity of a lifetime. Thank you to Zena Shapter for helping me shape the novel into something irresistible.

Of course, thank you to my family. My parents, Janet and Angelo, and my sister, Milena. Your unconditional love and support is a gift that I will forever be grateful for. To Grandma, for being my endless source of books—without that reading, I'd have no writing. Thank you Olivia, for being a treasure chest of ideas and my inexhaustible cheerleader; you have a solution to every problem! Thank you to my English teachers over the years, who have nurtured my creative development and allowed me to blossom, especially Cassandra Kennedy, who taught me that the greatest thing a book can be is a best friend. Thank you Tiya, who, when I was fifteen, reminded me that the best way to become a novelist is to write a novel. I took your advice! And to those who make self-doubt impossible—Emily, Lara, Hannah, Aleks, Pier, Seb, Ben, and Matisse. Your praise and confidence in me is priceless.

About the Author

AT 18 YEARS OF age, **Bruna Gomes** is already an award-winning writer. *How to Disappear* is her debut novel. She was born in Boston, Massachusetts, and grew up on the Northern Beaches of Sydney, Australia. She has received awards in various Sydney-based writing competitions, including the 2020 Mosman Youth Awards in Literature, and runner up in the Northern Beaches Young Writers Competition. When Bruna isn't writing, she enjoys traveling, reading, and time at the beach.

If you enjoyed reading this book,
please consider writing your honest review
and sharing it with other readers.

Many of our Authors are happy to participate in
Book Club and Reader Group discussions.
For more information, contact us at info@encirclepub.com.

Thank you,
Encircle Publications

For news about more exciting new fiction, join us at:

Facebook: www.facebook.com/encirclepub

Twitter: twitter.com/encirclepub

Instagram: www.instagram.com/encirclepublications

Sign up for Encircle Publications newsletter and specials:
eepurl.com/cs8taP